THE TRAGEDIES OF

NANA SERWAA

K.R. QUIAH

authorHOUSE®

AuthorHouse™
1663 Liberty Drive
Bloomington, IN 47403
www.authorhouse.com
Phone: 1 (800) 839-8640

Published by AuthorHouse 04/05/2017

ISBN: 978-1-5246-8482-2 (sc)
ISBN: 978-1-5246-8483-9 (hc)
ISBN: 978-1-5246-8481-5 (e)

Library of Congress Control Number: 2017904305

Print information available on the last page.

Disclaimer

Names of people and places, and events in this book are unreal; otherwise, they are geared toward entertainment purposes and do not in any way reflect or intend to reflect anything true; in cases of historical people and events and places and dates, the author seeks simply to create entertainment and does not seek in any way to tell or modify history or make an impression, other than for entertainment purposes.

DEDICATION

Written to the glory of God Almighty, Who puts great things in an earthen vessel

For my Darling, Kyrstie. For all your love, trust and motivation

To:

Kayden and Taryn, for teaching me to be a dad

David Seth Kwakwei Quartey, thanks for opening your home to me and being a father

My Grandpa, Brown Quiah (of blessed memories), for all the days you dragged me to school

My Papa and Mama, for giving me life and so much I have not room to list

My siblings, for your love and friendship and diverse support. Chiefly Larme, Brown, Roland and Quiah, for inspiring me in my writings

Dr. Lake and family, for your uncommon love

Cha Kee Vang & Rasmi Syonesa and family, for your profound love and support. Jack, thanks for all the efforts you put into the book cover

Conclusive Africa Senior Team: Joseph Swen, Kenneth Bracewell, Ochuko Kokofe, and Oscar Quiah Jr.

And, to all my family, friends and associates, who have been there for me, one way or another, to the fruition of this ambition

PROLOGUE

O MAN WAS SITUATED JUST ON the north-east of Ejura in Ashanti, with part of the city occupying portion of today's Brong Ahafo Region. In those days, Brong Ahafo to the north of Ashanti, Eastern Region to the east, Western Region to the south-west and Central Region to the south, all formed part of the Ashanti Kingdom. Oman was home to a small group of elite Akan speaking class. They were ruled by the Berimah family for over two centuries occupying 7 towns from north-east Ejura in the Ashanti Region eastward to Basa in Brong Ahafo Region.

In the late 17th and early 18th centuries when the great expansionist and founder of the Ashanti Kingdom Nana Osei Kofi Tutu consolidated the regions about Ashanti into a single kingdom, Oman, through a dialogue that lasted 3 years, remained autonomous. However, its kings will no longer call themselves by that title. Instead, they will be reverenced as chiefs – a clan head that paid tribute to the Ashanti throne based in Kumasi.

Otumfuo Nana Mensa Bonsu was made Ashanti king in 1874, after the forced abdication of Otumfuo Nana Kofi Karikari. Nine years on the throne, and Mensa Bonsu is also forced to abdicate the throne. The kingdom is plunged into civil war. Yaw Edusei, a member of the ruling Oyoko Dynasty, fights with the popular faction and distinguished himself by great military power and political maneuverings, ensuring the end of the 5 years civil war in 1888. The Council of Elders accepted the candidate who became Otumfuo Nana Kwaku Dua III Asamu and later renamed Otumfuo Nana Prempeh I. Now, the king and elders council will work to compensate many gallant men who stood to keep Ashanti together. Among them is Yaw Edusei, who is also of close kin to Otumfuo Nana Prempeh I.

CHAPTER I

OMAN IS WITNESSING THE FAREWELL ceremony of its chief's youngest child, Nana Serwaa Berimah. The chief, his wife and all of the people of Oman had expected a male child, and a 5th girl child in his sickness and ageing was the worst gift from the gods. It spelled one thing – the end of the Berimah royalty. Worse, she was the 5th child and '5' is considered an unlucky number. Yet Chief Berimah hopes to defy the odds. Peradventure a woman may rule Oman. The words of the priest at the time of Nana Serwaa's birth rings in his ears:

> *I see a woman whose one leg is planted among people of our kind, and the other leg among that of a strange people in a faraway place.*

The people and elders had sought to understand the meaning of what that saying might mean, but the Oracle spoke no more. He had said the much the gods had bade him. Off to his shrine he went, leaving a frustrated people anxious and perplexed.

Nana Berimah, chief of Oman and his wife had cared for their girl child. The gods, they believe, know better. They cannot be unfair, though men may often perceive them so when their expectations are cut short. Or rather seems. The gods see what men do not, know what men do not, and understand what men may never. All that may rightly be thought of the gods, but should they not speak in ways that ordinary men may comprehend? Should their speech or that of their messenger – the priest continually be in riddles making for confusion among the peoples? All these and more the great and aging man pondered as he lay in bed with his wife that night. He'd wished the gods visited him in a dream and informed his knowledge of small and great things to transpire in Oman in the years coming. He desired that at the least, the mercies of the gods would extend to his knowing of his successor.

In these days of hoar hairs and feeble knees, Nana Berimah knows that he must use his best of time and maneuverings to ensure his family continue as rulers of Oman. His four daughters and their husbands have only proven with his aging their gross incapability to rule the kingdom. Two of his daughters are married to men of foreign ethnicities and live away from Oman with their husbands. The other two husbands are a drunk and a rapist. And they have frequently been accused and guilty of extortion, while their wives have failed every test of their father. But Nana Berimah has grown too weak to take a serious action against them. Or perhaps, love for his daughters has clouded his judgement. His only hope is Nana Serwaa, in spite her sex and his ageing.

Off to Kumasi – the Royal Palace, Nana Serwaa Berimah must go. Perhaps she will become a wife of the to-be-crowned king of Ashanti. But to be the wife of any member of the royal family in Kumasi would be an honor, Nana Berimah had thought. So with his year old daughter he will attend the coronation of the new king of the Ashanti Kingdom, and present her duly.

The coronation of Ashanti's new king on March 26, 1888 marked a symbolic end of the civil war. Nana Serwaa Berimah was presented at the King Palace in Kumasi, the official residence of the Asantehene – king of the Ashanti Kingdom. Her father had believed against the traditional odds that his 5th child that failed to be a boy must have the strength of a male child – a somewhat greatness in her. Possibly the seer might have meant Kumasi, he reasoned. It may be a prosperous alliance may be forged between Oman and the throne in Kumasi because of her. But Otumfuo Nana Prempeh I requested that the child be cared for at home in Oman and returned in 15 years, when she had turned 16, the age of marriage for a royal Akan woman.

In the second year of his reign, Nana Prempeh I had his first major crisis on hand. An enemy force would be a better foe to plan for, a comparatively easy adversary against whom to find a solution. But Otumfuo and Ashanti are faced against the peril of nature. For several years the palm trees in the regions have been fast growing barren. And those were the years of the civil war. But now, there is peace and a king, yet there is scarcely pepper on any tree in the kingdom.

A strange pest has plagued every type of pepper in the region and spared not a single field or garden. The peoples are devastated. Meal is worthless without pepper for an Asante. Their best chance for pepper is Liberia, on the West African coastline.

But just how they get there pose a great challenge to Otumfuo and his council. This council is the emperor's council for strategy. It is made up of members of the elders' council, the cabinet, and the military advisory council. The council is challenged with devising the best route to Liberia. They consider distance, means of transportation, conditions such as weather, road and sea routes, and transporters, and more importantly the territories they must go through to the intended destination.

Pepper and palm trees are strangely barren the empire over. And while the priests and people look to the gods for answers and solutions, it is obligatory that Otumfuo and his council provide relief to these constraints the people are faced with. While the palm nut is a staple food for Asantes, the pepper spice goes with nearly every dish.

Two full days went by, with many hours spent deliberating possibilities to Liberia and back. On the third day and in the third and final meeting of the day, a youth in his early twenties stands up. He is a 5' 10", 171 pounder with Ashanti royal black complexion and thick black hair atypical of the ruling clan. It is past 4:00 PM and the sun is only just losing its intensity – the heat is somewhat felt in spite the cooling architecture of the palace. He had sat a couple hours without saying a word, and his voice is understandably heavy at the beginning. But just as he has proceeded from pleasantries or greetings, his voice becomes clearly adenoidal. Such a voice is common to the Ashanti royals.

His roundish-almond eyes scans the room almost as carefully as he speaks. Cautiously he dismisses the options of cameling and walking west-southward to Liberia; the chance of war with peripheral Mande ethnic groups such as the Gouro would be easily provoked. Gouro tribes were at wars with Baole and Krou tribes that are of kin to the Asantes. An over 1,000 troop going through the regions would imply nothing but Ashanti war against the Gouros. And against the unfriendly rains.

Cameling and walking south and then traveling by ship to the Republic of Liberia seems feasible. But just how? It will take negotiations for Ashanti troop and merchants to enter British controlled Cape Coast and arrange travel, or it may require the force of arms. Yaw Edusei vigilantly dispelled the notion that the British will hold no negotiations with Asante, that the only possibility was war. "It will strangulate the kingdom should they engage in a war any time soon" Yaw Edusei said in a fruity voice, and yet appealing gesture as he looked approvingly to Otumfuo. "Of what good will a well of gold be compared with an Ashanti life" he spoke, looking at faces in the room as though requiring an answer. That latter statement especially goes to council members that think it too expensive to pay out gold to the British, forgetting that war comes at the very cost of gold, and additional and more significantly, human life.

The expedition troop they drastically reduced and increased the merchants, as counter-proposed by Nana Yaw Edusei. In a week's time from that afternoon, Nana Edusei and the chief royal ambassador led an expedition comprising 300 troop, 100 merchants, 40 sailors, 2 physicians, 6 elders, a priest, and a seer. They successfully negotiated a to and fro entry through British territories, and acquired the use of 3 British vessel among others.

Within 3 months the Ashanti expedition was concluded. Their mission was successful, but not without problems. They were involved in a few small wars. Those few times they were mistaken for an invading force, and each time, before their mission was understood by the local peoples, they had lost members of the expedition. In all of that, Yaw Edusei showed courage and resilience, and proved himself; not merely as a soldier, but as a negotiator the young royal showed himself apt. The largely favorable report Otumfuo Nana Prempeh I received about Nana Edusei impressed the King, that he made him his chief military commander.

In 1894, some 6 years after the coronation of the Asantehene Otumfuo Nana Prempeh I, the last male head of the ruling line of the Berimah family in Oman had passed unto his ancestors. The political state of Oman is fragile. It has been for a long time. But Ashanti is too powerful, even careful, to allow Oman to fall into succession dispute. At least such a dispute or war would not go on long. The head of the local chiefs would preside over affairs, until a decision was made by Otumfuo on Oman.

Today, considering Yaw Edusei's childless circumstances coupled with his services to the throne and empire, Otumfuo can find no better man for the Oman royal girl. He did not think it twice and is certain his decision will pay well for Yaw and

Ashanti at large. It may seem a thing to scorn, that Yaw should await years and another marriage before he should have a child of his own, but everyone present could trust that Otumfuo knew well, if not better. As an heir to the throne, you are trained as a counselor. You take case studies on various subjects including marriage, which poses several challenges ranging from infidelity to barrenness to irresponsible parenting. And the diverse solutions in the lessons are all predicated on Ashanti customs and traditions. If a woman fails to give her husband children, the man may take unto himself another wife; by his discretion he may keep or put away the barren wife. These men present at King Palace know too well that time will come by fast, and Yaw Edusei would scarcely have transcended the youthful barrier – 35 years, according to Ashanti definition of male youth.

But for Ashanti's interest, the king of Oman had passed unto his ancestors untimely! Otumfuo Nana Prempeh I had hoped that the Omanhene (Nana Berimah) married out his daughter before his demise. Yaw is Nana Prempeh's best hope to finally bring Oman under absolute Ashanti rule. Otumfuo reassures himself that his plan for Oman is the will of the gods, but concedes that the events and details are their workings! He will simply keep an eagle's eye on the small kingdom Ashanti has left autonomous for many years. It is 9 years until the Berimah girl is of age to marry. Until then, Kumasi will join Oman in the funeral arrangements and observances for Omanhene Nana Berimah.

Shortly after the funeral processions of Omanhene Nana Berimah, the Ashanti Kingdom and its rulers and peoples turn their focus on celebration. Odwera is one of the biggest festivals in Ashanti. It is the biggest religious annual festival celebrated by the entire peoples of the kingdom. It is a period of forgiveness of trespasses, and freedom and blessings into the New Year. The Asante believes in sin, and even the Otumfuo – the head of

Ashanti could lose the favor of the Gods and be stripped to an ordinary citizen if his acts were unkind and base toward humans and his sins grievous before the gods. Odwera is like a Passover everyone – commons and royals hope to celebrate through. In essence, it is the festival of renewing and the bridge into the New Year. Ashanti is a land of many rituals and Odwera produces no fewer than the other grand festivals celebrated by Asantes kingdomwide.

September is here and the new moon approaches. The messages of festivities are transmitted daily by the royal drummers. Citizens including chiefs will leave their divisions and towns and villages and come to the royal capital of Kumasi. The royal high priest, not the king, will be the center of attraction. But Ashanti could never seize from admiring the Otumfuo. Especially not Nana Prempeh I. He is young and handsome, gay and generous and yet has the wisdom and firmness admired by even his council. However, he will be that great side attraction the Otumfuos often are during the Odwera Festival. His high priest will take the center stage and officiate the festival.

Ashanti is fully represented at Odwera 1895. All of its chiefs and leaders are present in the square of the royal palace. They are not merely the guests of Otumfuo Nana Prempeh I; everyone, including the king, is guest of the gods, or rather lightly, the high priest who leads them through the cleansing rites. But this Odwera is surprisingly overshadowed by the high priest's alarming prophecy. In fact, the news is soon out of the palace square into all of the city, and Kumasi is stunned. Ashanti is stupefied and its citizens look to each other, unable to speak more than a few words. Once the priest did speak the words. Now it is no more than a whisper even among the elders and members of the king's council. None can openly repeat that Otumfuo Nana Prempeh I, head of all the Akan tribes that formed the great Ashanti Kingdom and Custodian of the Ashanti people, would be taken into exile. Ashanti began to mourn. Even more terrifying was the fact that the priest predicted it would happen so soon: "Ashanti will see three full moons, and the fourth, well before before it is full, Otumfuo Nana Prempeh I will be taken into a foreign land."

Otumfuo Nana Prempeh I is king of Ashanti. The king could not be afraid. At least he could reveal no sign of fear before his subjects. However, Nana Prempeh I is fearless. He believes that whatever happens was the will of the gods and he was too experienced, in spite his somewhat youthful age, to resist or doubt the words of the gods. He had waved the chief priest to continue the festival when everyone expected the prophecy signified the end. And when all of the rituals and traditions were complete and Odwera done, he retired to his chambers where none was to enter till the king's waking hour the next morning. Usually the king would party and discuss with his guests late night during Odwera. But not tonight. Nana Prempeh I is only king of Ashanti, not a god. He is, plainly put, a human.

Every one may become fearful at some point in life. The Otumfuo may have become. But to entertain fear was to succumb to it, and the head of this great people knew the implications of that. So he braved the waves of fear during the night and awoke the next day the fearless and gay king his people knew him for. His first meeting among many was with Nana Yaw Edusei, and the last with his wives and children. He was leaving soon. There may not be vacuum in Kumasi because the British would seize power here. But the kingdom must be strengthened in every Division for the peoples' sake. Now, there is a seat in the herd-rich Oman for which war was breeding, and it is in the king's sole power to appoint an Obirempon (Big Man).

Yaw Edusei must go over to Oman as Obirempon. He will govern Oman under the kingdom until the next Asantehene – Ashanti king and council make a permanent or lasting decision. The king spoke decisively and his words were largely orders than suggestions or petitions to say the least. Yet Yaw Edusei is tempted to resist the king's commands. Why the head of Ashanti should be taken into exile like an ordinary peasant. At the least, he thought, there must be a fight. But he could only think it, for the Otumfuo's eyes were piercing within that seeming smiling face. Yaw Edusei paid homage to his master and left his presence. A new office and a wife and life await the warrior in Oman. He has 60 days to prepare himself and leave for his new station.

Barely 2 months after Nana Yaw Edusei left Kumasi for Oman - in January of 1896, had the British expedition force entered Kumasi. To the utmost dismay of his council and the army, Otumfuo Nana Prempeh I had just two hours ago delivered this speech before members of the royal family and various officials of the kingdom:

> *"The Queen-mother, members of the royal house, paramount chiefs, our wise council of elders, and every Asante that listen to me at this moment, and that shall hear of this moment:*
>
> *When our forefathers, Nana Obiri Yeboah and Nana Osei Tutu I established this great empire, it was not about themselves. Greed had no place in their hearts, but that the pertaining of the highest and best in world society belonged to the one that has an Ashanti blood. They placed our people ahead of themselves, and the gods of our ancestors and our great ethnicity provided for their various necessities, and Ashanti prospered in their care.*
>
> *The way of the gods have been known to us through our priests from the foundation of this empire. The gods' will had been no secret a business when Ashanti was in distress and need. And when our progenitors understood and obeyed these, the land prospered in*

their hands; but when they went contrary, Ashanti suffered, from the greatest even to the least.

Now, answer me, great peoples of our lands. Can Ashanti be conquered? Shall the land of the Golden Stool not be protected by the same gods that established it through the hands of his great priest Okomfo Anokye and king, Nana Osei Tutu I? Far be such disbelief in the gods and defamation of their veritable nature.

But though the way of the gods are sometimes strange, we must do according to their will. The gods have willed that the head of Ashanti should be taken into exile by the white man. Sooner than you can expect, they will arrive here in Kumasi, and may it be without a fight. These foreign people will not accomplish this by their own strength, but by the will of the gods. The gods require us to be peaceful, and do as bade. And though your spirit may be broken, may your hearts be cheered in this: the same gods that lead my feet into exile have also promised to bring me back and reestablish the kingdom through me.

My mother, do not weep. My wife, do not cry for me. Ashanti, we mourn for the dead, but the living we must celebrate."

The Ashantehene is accustomed to complete silence from his people when he speaks. But today it appears everything is business unusual. The weeping women will not heed to summons from council men and family members to keep quiet or seize from weeping; not even the words of Nana Prempeh I could prevail here. And here, in this weeping and speaking and comforting, news of the British arrival reaches the palace. The king's directives were quickly about the city, as the crier (announcer) publicized it through drumming and foot messengers.

The Ashanti king retired to his chambers, dressed in an Ashanti royal traveling attire, and returned to the main palace hall where his nobles waited on him, along with the British Gold Coast governor William Maxwell and two of his assistants, that arrived a couple hours after their expedition force peacefully marched through Kumasi and posted outside the King Palace.

Then, contrary to popular historical account that the Ashanti emperor and other ruling members of the empire were arrested, Otumfuo Nana Prempeh I presented himself to Governor Maxwell, and 12 officials including council men and other chiefs (for the council was made up largely of chiefs) volunteered to accompany the emperor. Like a sheep led to the slaughter, the gods presented as it was, the Ashanti nobles into the hand of their British adversaries. And in that moment Ashanti power waxed cold, as gloom descended upon its peoples.

Ashanti's head may be smitten, but circumstances are like its peoples would say of themselves, "we are great because we enjoy the highest providence and endure the severest chastisement; and now, though fallen, always we rise." Therefore the people are unbroken in spirit, though troubled.

As the days went by and the news traveled far and wide, many were broken to the heart, but one man was torn apart. It was Nana Yaw Edusei, Governor of Oman. The news bearer reached the governor's house – the palace of Oman, at 11:45PM. The governor had already withdrawn to his bed chambers when his chief aide hit the door with coded knocks. The governor, upon hearing a guest was in from Kumasi, knew full well that something was amiss. But somewhat unsurprising. For Yaw had spent that entire day without food, safe for kola and tea. His soul was gravely troubled within, and he delved into thinking all day but failed to fathom the cause.

As he entered the hall, the news bearer bowed himself in greetings, then casted himself to the floor with scarcely hands to protect his frail body. With a loud cry that could be heard in every space of the palace and beyond, he said the words of Otumfuo Nana Prempeh I and other nobles' exile. The governor crashed onto the floor. The king was not only of close kin to him, but in truth, his younger brother. Ashanti calls the first cousin sibling. And as Yaw sat on the floor and sobbed, he reflected on the years when they were younger, and he used to care for Nana Prempeh, who is 2 years younger than himself. He had rescued the boy from drowning in a river; and saved him from falling into a swamp as they hung unto bush ropes to take a short cut to their destination. But on both occasions, Yaw reminds himself, Nana Prempeh called out for his help. This time, he had sent him away from Kumasi before Yaw should think of helping him. Yaw Edusei, now turned on his back, lifted his hands into the air and shouted "Prempeh! You tied these hands I swore to protect you with. The prince of princes is led like an ordinary man of some vagabond tribe. And our people; who will guide them?" So did Yaw lament the fall of the Ashanti kingdom and Otumfuo. And though now he will sober himself, because of his wife and wife to be Nana Serwaa and the peoples that stand around, Yaw will require a while to heal. But only a while, for though human he is, the man is an Ashanti warrior. The warrior's code dictated that a person see all circumstances as the will of the gods, and find and celebrate the silver lining within.

Gladly the warrior Yaw Edusei accepted Otumfuo's choice of Nana Serwaa as his second wife. He could not refuse her because it was the king's order. And he was glad he accepted her because she is stunningly beautiful. When he first saw her she was only a toddler. Now she is nearly 16 years and her beauty is vivid in the warrior's eyes. However, he reckons the time is months away, and momentarily he will require the warmth and services of his barren wife Nana Yaa. She gave him no children, but she warms his bed and administrates the home. Yaw Edusei could at least appreciate her, though his love for her had waxed cold.

When Yaw Edusei's parents had married for him a woman 2 years his senior, they did not foresee she will be of snare to a son who will excel in everything in life. As a royal, he was privileged to attend school. He was one of the brightest kids and versed in all subjects that his fame was about Kumasi and within the walls of the royal palace. He went on to excel in military training and service, and became a great pride of his family and kinsmen. For the boy could master anything. But unfortunately, he could not get his wife pregnant. Or rather, everything fell easy to him but his wife giving him a child. It steals from the greatness of Yaw Edusei. And worse, it has been 19 years, and she has not conceived. Their sins have been atoned for, more than once, and various other measures taken but to no avail. Yet to put her away was to risk everything. For she belonged to the house of Mampong, the second ruling family in Ashanti.

Oman had lost its last male member – chief of the clan and peoples, to a natural cause of death. But that had happened rather timely to prevent the Otumfuo's forcing him out to bring Oman directly under Ashanti. It was believed that Oman was giving much less than it ought to in tribute to the throne in Kumasi. It was arrived at that the Berimahs will be forced out and a new leader, even Yaw Edusei, will govern the land and have the stool – the throne in Kumasi, have its rightful due. But a second and secret meeting took place between Otumfuo, Yaw Edusei and a close friend and advisor of the king. The secret meeting concluded that Yaw Edusei should marry the Berimah girl and bring Oman directly under Ashanti. The marriage, for Nana Prempeh I, is the undeniable smooth path. But fate made a smoother business of it with the early natural death of the chief of Oman. Mampong will understand that to secure Oman under Ashanti, Yaw Edusei – their son in-law must marry from the royal house of Oman. But this was, in truth, to the intent that Yaw Edusei should have children and become a real man. For a man without children, particularly a male child, could not be considered great.

Oman has a new leader and new additions to the royal family. But the family is nothing for these anxious people to become relaxed about. Yaw Edusei and his wife, servants and guards; that did not fit for a happy ruling family. A child, especially a male child, would gladden the hearts of these people. They cared less that the governor was not a descendant of Oman, for he was also an Ashanti and a servant and kin of Otumfuo Nana Prempeh I. But all the ordinary people here care to see children in the royal house, a boy particularly, regardless if such a one will become ruler of Oman someday.

June 18, 1903, Oberimpon Nana Yaw Edusei, Governor of Oman, is seated at a wedding feast. He is marrying for the second time, but today it is different. When he married his first wife, it was a simple ceremony where only members of their immediate families were present. But today, there are hundreds of people gathered in the city square to celebrate the wedding of a stranger. Though a non-native of Oman, the people at large respect and admire Yaw Edusei for his impartial judgement, innovative administration and prosperous management of the kingdom. Respect and admiration must suffice for Yaw Edusei. He cannot expect that these people will love him; all of their love seems to be reserved for one of the male children they hope, Nana Serwaa, the royal bride today, should bare him. After a lengthy but lavished ceremony in which all of the guests feasted sufficiently, the crowning and long awaited moment arrives. The couple kneel before the high priest and the latter rain words of blessing upon them, to which the audience joyously chanted "may it so be." But the loudest chant was reserved for the blessing of sons, and the chant "may it so be" echoed Oman over like a thunderstorm or the rush of mighty waters that the earth under Yaw Edusei and his bride trembled. The gods must show him beneficence.

Nana Serwaa's thick black hair is ornamented with gold and colorful beads. Her usually styled threaded hair glitters in this tropical day from traditionally refined shear butter. The pupil of her eyes reflect in the bright day, and is set in irises of burnished black on sclera as white as snow. As for her skin, they are soft at look and feel, an onyx Sub-Saharan complexion. A slim long nose slants slightly at the nostrils and sits between her protruding eyes and above an elegant half-full set of lips. Her stunningly gorgeous face that would confuse some for a diamond-shape and others for an oval-shape is today painted with traditional symbols. Her expressive length neck, finely set in lovely ringed skin, drips with elaborate golden necklace and colorful traditional beads. And her extensive hand – from arm to wrist to fingers displayed the richness of Oman in gold and traditional beaded jewelries. Her entire 5.7ft figure, at 16, is a spectacle.

To omit description of her breasts and hips and legs, even briefly, would be to desecrate the immortality of beauty. For, as the ancient saying goes, "beauty is immortality." Her breasts stood pomp, full and round and soft, lodged in a golden yellow Kente cloth with leafy green and ruby red threads woven in it. Her hips and bums were impressively animated and wrapped about with another piece of the same cloth she donned her breast with. Her wrapper extended from her waist and landed a few inches above her knees, allowing her dazzling legs adorned with richly colorful beads to be seen and seize the gaze of onlookers.

She is the typical beauty of a maiden Akan (Oman) girl, but Nana Serwaa is much more than just another girl. Her face and figure makes it impossible for anyone to look on her just once; one had to look at her again and again. A sight to behold is the only hope of the Berimah Royal House of Oman. And her manners are no less than her beauty. She is graceful and courtly, as are the norm of one who grows up in a palace. Her impeccable manners and grace makes her the symbol of the Berimah royalty and an example every girl in Oman strives toward being. But though courtesies may be learned, true royalty is innate.

And little is remembered that on this day in 1888, Nana Ama Bosomtwe brought into this world a 5th girl child – Nana Serwaa. Her birthday is overshadowed by her marriage. Even she cares less about it. It is not a day Oman will ever care about, except she gives them a boy child to continue the rule of its great king, her father. 16 years ago this day spelled doom in Oman, but today, her groom, Governor Yaw Edusei is bent on changing the fortune of the date. And that she welcomes and throws in her all. The pair are doubtless that children, particularly male children, will be born into their union, and that Oman's hopes will be established.

CHAPTER II

WITH GREAT BRITAIN HAVING ANNEXED the Ashanti Empire, or rather, the capital Kumasi, there are now frequent wars in the region. The Asantes are no easy people to pay tribute to the British. Britain would have to enter each Division or city and build a forte as done in Kumasi before these pride Africans should submit and tributes be exacted from them. Hence, with wars sparsely about Ashanti between clans and cities and divisions, the British are inclined to concentrate on the throne home of Kumasi.

March 1904, about nine months after Yaw Edusei married Nana Serwaa Berimah in a royal pomp, Oman is attacked. The enemy is less of a conquering army and more of a raiding band. They had laid waist the large city-division of Ejura, just west of Oman, plundering items of gold, children and women. The battle drum is heard at the four corners of the city, but there is hardly any time for the officers to muster. A quick command is given by the governor, who himself for the first time leads these people to war.

Yaw Edusei concentrated the best of his forces on the western border where the assault was initiated. He ordered 100 men led by a veteran marksman who had fought in 30 battles to guard the women and children eastward. The man has fought for Oman, for the Ashanti Kingdom against the British twice, and the neighboring city and village states contracted his service from time to time. His fame was far and wide beyond Oman and into all of Ashanti, even unto the southern cape and across the Volta River on the east. His name was Kwame Boakye.

To the Omanians, Kwame Boakye out of the main battle seemed a grave error by the governor. But none could question Yaw Edusei. He was not a spoon-fed governor but a warrior, and that all the men of war knew. Still they found it strange why another great warrior – Kwame Boakye didn't join them. The battle on the western border lasted over 5 hours. Oman had lost hundreds of its sons, but they had the upper hand, having put a near-thousand of the barbarians to the death. As Oman fought in the final two hours, at the very point when the battle was swiftly going Oman's way, they realized Kwame Boakye in the fight. Yes, it was Boakye here fighting to save Oman, the only place he calls home. Anxiety was at the height and none dared ask why he was here in the battle at the western border. But soon, the battle was done. Kwame Boakye had proved himself a hero and a warrior once more. But the men of Oman learned quite well that Yaw Edusei was indeed a warrior. He lived up to the fame they have heard of him. He fought for Oman like a true prince, and these men of war will immortalize him, if even in their hearts.

Oman, as it goes, did not win in the battle. They might have inflicted many deaths on the barbarians. But to the east of Oman, when Kwame Boakye and his 100 men led the women and children and elderlies to safety, they bumped into a near 700 men of arms. They were of the same barbarian band. The barbarians attack a major exit on the far side of a city or town, and have a large number of its men in the main opposite direction to intercept women and children that are likely the ones to flee battle. And there were over a thousand five hundred women and children and older people that could move somewhat swiftly, fleeing the battle. Many of the old people stayed at home.

Kwame Boakye and his men were no match to this second arm of the raiding troop. And he was no fool. He did not survive 30 battles by fighting always. He is alive, after all, because he knows when to fight and when to retreat. Maybe also, he knows when to surrender, though that is something this warrior is yet to have done. 5 years ago, the only woman around when he fought against the British was herself the leader of the Ashanti Army. She was Yaa Asantewaa, Queen Mother of Ejisu. The Ashanti fought bravely against the British in spite the latter's sophistication in arms. But on that fateful day the Asantes were beaten and Yaa Asantewaa and many other Ashanti royals and soldiers were taken captive. But Kwame Boakye refused to surrender, evading capture.

Today they were no warriors by his side but women and children and grannies and old men, safe a paltry 100 men. To fight the raiders is to risk the lives of these vulnerable people. And how else could he save them? They were his responsibility, and by the Ashanti warrior code he must protect them above his life. A split second decision was arrived at: He would not fight against the raiding band, at least not now. But he would not surrender. Otherwise, how else could he win back the people if they are taken? For they will be taken. It was a hard fact he had to reconcile with. He urged the people to remain peaceful and not resist the raiders. He promised that he will return to free them. So swiftly Kwame Boakye and his men fled for the bushes. And to their faint disbelief, they were not pursued.

The leader of the raiding band was himself present. He knew the task of carrying so many people and cattle away safely was herculean. Now he sees what is well over a thousand women, children and aged people. He will need all of his men alive and fit. His custom is to drive the people far away from their home as possible, and select the best of them to carry to his kingdom. The others he leaves to decide their own fate. He is a realistic man who knows the sheer difference between possibility and impossibility. He led 3000 men on this expedition. A first group is headed home with thousands of cattle and women and children, aside gold and other valuables. He is hopeful to do the same here. The unit of his band that attacked the western part of Oman is to bring out the cattle and other loots, while he is to intercept and carry away human cargo.

Buka, the raiding band leader is a 6 feet giant of a man. He has the face of a prince, though the leader of a raiding band. Many times, people thought he was kind. But Buka was only clever. He retains what is safe to, and parts with what is terribly coveted by his men and dangerous to his retaining. Thus, Buka has successfully managed his army and governed his kingdom "Wa" as he likes to call his country, for most of his adult life to date. He will lead the second and final group of this expedition back home with cargo of humans. He will carry away even the royal house captive, but Oman will keep its cattle. For Buka's men on the western flank of Oman were crushed while a minute remnant managed to escape during the heat of the battle. And, Yaw Edusei remains alive.

Buka was 10 years old when his father Suka (The Spider), perished. Unlike Buka, Suka sat at home and ordered raids and battles. He used vicious psycho-tactics to keep his men loyal, or rather submitted, to him. He pit every one of his top soldiers against one another that he became each one's trusted friend and sole dependent. Suka adopted his name from an ancient story which tells that spider is the king of all living creatures. Indeed, he was an opportunist – a true spider. He went nowhere but had everything brought unto him. How he loved to repeat these words to himself: "A king is served!" Suka so hypnotized himself with those words that the only things he ever did were visit the bed chambers of his wives and fed his own meal. Three female servants ran his bath.

But Buka was quite unlike his father. He was called Raka (The King) by his father, but before he was 16 and crowned the head of his peoples, he had adopted Buka (The Lion). He was a soldier and a skilled leader. He was everything good and fit to the pleasing of his subjects, but a man is never without fault or weakness. While his father had married 7 wives and had many concubines, Buka took one wife and would know no other woman. She was the bride of his youth and the love of his life. To him it was honest and more favorable to take one wife and spare other women the opportunity of having their own husbands. Yet certain of his subjects took that for weakness. Their rationale was that if ever that wife should pass on to their ancestors before Buka, their king would become incapable of ruling the kingdom - sick with grief. The Wa-Zangan nobles are of the opinion that it is most unfit for a man to love, for even the love of a peasant may enslave a king.

No sooner had the Omanian warriors reassembled themselves in the square of the city than the arrival of the priest. There before the mighty warriors of Oman and the governor, the priest is given audience. In times of war, when this people go to battle, they first consult the priest. Today Oman was attacked. There was no time for consultation. However, at this decisive point in time, the priest is away from his shrine and in the city square to deliver the oracle of the gods: Oman must not pursue the raiders. It is the will of the gods that the queen – Nana Serwaa, is taken away. With those words the men of Oman are stayed from another battle. Yaw Edusei, though, is most unhappy.

It was nearly a week's journey to Wa-Zanga, the kingdom of Buka. Careful considerations were made of the captives and pickings were done. The captives were bruised and sored, thirsty and hungry. Of 150 women and children picked for the journey, 6 died of starvation and dehydration. 144 made it to Buka's capital following a daily ration of under half pint of water, and a piece of corn, cassava or whatever uncooked-edible crop they came across on the way. Their captors were careful not to feed them much, and not more than once. However, they recognized the princess and newly wedded bride of the governor of Oman. She rode on horse back alongside Buka, guided by one of his lieutenants. And Nana Serwaa ate at Buka's table throughout the journey.

The final captives that reached Wa-Zanga comprised females of ages 14 to 30. Nana Yaa, Yaw Edusei's First Wife, was spared for this reason. The selection is based on youthfulness, strength and look. The captives will be sold into slavery and their masters would use them for various purposes which included prostitution to generate revenue for the master. Still, others, though few, of Wa-Zanga bought captives and married them. So few because the strict laws of Buka's kingdom prohibited children born of foreign women from inheriting lands and other properties. Though, in essence, the law applied only to none-royals

Today, Buka arrives home. His counselors have decided that he takes a second wife. The wisdom of the counsel was audacious and yet ingenuous. Their king would be spared the guilt of marrying a woman of Wa-Zanga, since he was of the conviction that every citizen needed his or her own spouse. Here in Wa-Zanga today, is a stranger, but one with a noble blood and fit for their leader. They had suggested it to their king and band head early on their journey back home. But the words of Suka his father echoed in his ears: "First things first." He had the task of leading his troop and loot home safely. That, and nothing else was of significance until they were safely home. And this they understood. They always revered his wisdom.

The queen of Wa-Zanga is beautiful and of royal lineage. She is smart and skilled at vices. A little over 10 years ago, her older

sister Maiyama was the proposed bride of Buka. Under a week to their wedding and still in their father's house, Kalima the now queen of Wa-Zanga, paid a Malam – medicine man to prevent her sister's marriage to Buka. She had conferred with the malam - Zaduka that death was not an option, since it might become too obvious. Moreover, the death of a royal required a priest to divine the cause. Kalima could not risk such. She would rather have her sister made sick, a case which the elders would consider natural, a fate from the Gods for her trespass, a prevention of a worse fate or, consequentially, another of the royal house is the gods' chosen for marriage to the Wa-Zangan prince.

At Kalima's request the Malam casted a spell – a skin disease on her sister that looked somewhat like leprosy. Not even their mother could look on Maiyama. And Kalima, not sure what sickness it was that the spell would bring, is stunned and has taken to regret. This was graver and more painful than she had anticipated. She will live with her regret, but it is her father that bears the greater or rather perhaps immediate trouble of facing the wise and dreaded Buka.

The Midwestern Kingdom enjoyed the peace it did owing much to the wisdom of Kalima's father - its king. He had forged alliances on every side of his kingdom. Some of these allies were public, but many were private for fear of provoking another ally. To the mightiest of his allies he would say of himself and his people, "we are your subjects, fit and ready for that which is expedient for your great pleasure that is guided by the highest wisdom." And to the weakest of his allies he reassured: "You are not without strength because of the size of your land, neither because of your population, nor because of your cattle or wealth; your weakness is dictated by your decision to stand alone." And he demonstrated this by holding in his hand a single broom straw and breaking it without an effort, and again holding together a good bunch of straws and unsuccessfully attempting to break even a straw off the bunch.

Today his wisdom must bear than at no other times. He must answer young King Buka the cause of the sudden cancellation of the latter's wedding. Buka was young and strong, and much wiser and patient than his years. The gods, it is said in Wa-Zanga, had given him the three spirits. Wa-Zangans believe that three spirits controlled all the powers of the human world, and only once in every 300 years did they choose a body on earth to occupy. And in the fierceness of their anger against King Suka, they had killed him and chose his son. But if wisdom is any way in years, Buka could at least expect that the hoar haired – King Atuba of the Midwestern Kingdom, would fitly answer him. After all, he had summoned the old king who was a close friend and ally of his father.

King Atuba began by telling Buka the legendary story of the sun and moon's broken engagement. Pointing Buka to the Sun near setting in the east, he began his tale:

Many years ago, when Time was only an infant, the Great One thought to provide for its correction. Sun and Moon were chosen to guide her. Sun by day and Moon by night, each in due season.

Sun burned with anger from dawn to dusk – till his duty was accomplished for the day. He agonized about his love for Moon whom he had scarcely seen. He had intended to have the hand of Moon in matrimony, but broke his engagement with her out of frustration of not seeing her in a 366 day cycle.

"My son" called the old wise king to Buka as the two royals faced each other, "Maiyama is not your wife. Your destinies are incompatible. The gods have reduced her to a state unfit for even a peasant. Her disease is worse, the priest tells me, than leprosy. Look, I beseech of you in your kindest temperance and highest wisdom, upon the daughters of the kingdom of your subject, beginning with my own house, and take whichever damsel or as many as pleases your royal appeal." To this request the young king conceded, and on the set day visited the Midwestern Kingdom.

Kalima was beautiful, much so than her elder sister Maiyama. To look upon her was a pleasure of feasting one's eyes on one of the grandest splendors of creation, and the boldest and smartest damsel countrywide. She wore her beauty with grace and her intelligence with confidence. Her introversive spirit made her the kingdom's favorite of three princesses born to King Atuba. Buka could pick no other when he had set his eyes on this princess and made a greeting exchange with her.

King Buka's visit to the Midwestern kingdom concluded with his proposed marriage to Princess Kalima. She was the ultimate maiden in the entire kingdom. The gods only could have thought otherwise. Not a soul could see that beyond all of Kalima's noble qualities was a heart and soul of the devil, safe the Malam Zadukai and the maid Sairi.

On the set date, King Buka took the hand of princess Kalima in marriage. And to tell of their marriage – a 7 day ceremony and celebration, not a soul in the kingdom did the dainties of the royal table escape. Present were the priests and chiefs, elders and councilmen, members of the royal family and the ordinary citizenry, the latter among which came Zadukai – the malam Princess Kalima had used. There were prestigious royal guests which included Samori Toure of the Wassulu Empire and an emissary from the Ashanti Empire.

Queen Kalima's chief maid is spouse to one of Buka's trusted vassals. The vassal had told her all about the plan to take a second wife for Buka. The proposed bride is a royal captive – wife of Nana Yaw Edusei, Obirempong of Oman. But the men responsible for this plan will have a stern price to pay. For the queen requites favor and disfavor with equally astronomical measures. She left Zadukai the Malam six ounces of gold richer; from the newest and least of the maids in the palace at the Western Kingdom, Saira was promoted the chief handmaid for masterminding the plot that saw Maiyama bewitched and Kalima, queen of Wa-Zanga. With Kalima and Saira having perfected the shrewd art of vice, and Zadukai less than a sun's rising and setting away, there is scarcely anything impossible for this team.

Now, alone with Queen Kalima in her personal chamber, Saira the chief maid makes known all she has heard from Buka's general. She is unsurprised to see her mistress is almost unperturbed. Kalima was only a teenager when she arrived in Wa-Zanga, but these ten years have come with adversities and glitches she could scarcely have imagined or planned for. Through it all, she has become a woman too hardened and too grounded to be moved, and so much hardened for the needles of pain to penetrate. She scarcely is hopeful of a happier life; she has given the king no male child to succeed him, neither a female child to cheer him. What better could the gods make of her or give her further. Her position as a queen is all she has, and this estate she intends to defend at a priceless cost.

Three days are gone by since his return from the plunder of Oman, and Buka informs his wife the queen that Nana Serwaa, the royal captive, will lodge in the palace. She will reside in what was his childhood chamber on the east side of the palace. He has mentioned only that it is unfit to host her anywhere out of the palace (as had been for two nights) in consideration of the status of the captive woman. But Queen Kalima knows too well that the king is predisposed to do as he pleases, and that the gratification of his bed pleasures has long found out her inadequacies. She would not question her lord, neither plead with him, nor hope that the obvious is spared her; she is too inclined to open a cup of suspicion when there is, directly, none, and too experienced to insinuate infidelity of the king; Kalima knows that guided action is her only chance to save her face and keep her estate.

Nana serwaa's first night in the palace was her best day since she was taken captive. In truth, except for the fact of her captivity, the being away from her husband, family and land of nativity, the abundance of everything here is more than she had known at any time in Oman. Such abundance and richness in food for even the least fortunate or poor, opulence of gorgeous garments dazzling with pure gold and precious stones of varying colors worn by the nobles, and splendor in architectures, she certainly experienced only in Kumasi at King Palace. Undoubtedly much more.

Nevertheless, this is little Wa-Zanga. The peoples of the chiefdoms and kingdoms around for the most, have heard only the worst of this kingdom and its lord. Rumor has it that he is an uncivilized barbarian, uncultured and uncourt, and that he and his people live in bushes and caves. And worst, they are heinous slave drivers and traders who eat the dead of their captives. Moreover, there are horrifying stories of spite and vice of Wa-Zanga women. But these past days have altered greatly, if not changed fully, Nana Serwaa's ill-informed knowledge of the little kingdom and its people. And tonight will obliterate the excesses of her misconception as she dines with the king and queen.

Seated at the great table were King Buka, Queen Kalima, Nana Serwaa, two of Buka's top generals and their wives, and finally, the widower and chief advisor of Buka – Negutu the Wise. Here is the smallest and frequently used of three dining rooms the palace boasts. To talk of its splendor would consume the time and may threaten the flow of events which are pressing at this dinner. And of the richness and glamor and sophistication of the garments worn by the diners, permit me escape, for the sake of brevity and the satisfaction of greater curiosity.

Everyone knew what to expect at the table. Princess Kalima expected the official announcement of her husband's new bride, and perhaps a discussion of the following formalities. But, this cannot be said of Nana Serwaa. If she expected anything, it was another experience of Wa-Zanga cuisine and hospitality. Oh, and folklores from a member or few at the table; for it was a way of the Wa-Zangan's to compliment a dinner banquet with tales. However, in the royal house of Wa-zanga, important matters are reserved for the close of meal. Certain discussions may cause one to lose appetite or forgo meal. Quintessentially, you never send out a person invited to the table hungry.

So when the various sections of meals were served and done with, and the table cleared of tableware safe for Egyptian crafted gold cups used for the serving of guna – the strange tea, King Buka signaled discussion underway. One of the generals, who was the royal treasurer, speaking in fluent Kosai, gave account of the king's estate, particularly a report of the recent expedition. He spoke Kosai because it was the royal language, spoken only by members of the upper class. The widely spoken language – Kosini, was spoken in various kingdoms and countries nearby, and it was acknowledged that Nana Serwaa and all of the Berimah's royal house in Oman spoke Kosini. Furthermore, military commanders gave commands to their subjects in Kosai. When the treasurer had completed his report, it passed to the next general, who was commander of the army. He spoke carefully, almost emotionless and with hardly any gesture. Yet, within half the time spent by the treasurer, the commander of the army had given report on the state of the army, with emphasis on the recent expedition, and concluded with preparation plans for near future missions. Now, it is the turn of the much awaited Emusheguta (His Eminence) Netugu the Wise.

Revered for his wisdom, and now with senses heightened by the guna, so much is expected of Netugu. The proud son of Wa-Zanga greets the king and queen, and the table guests, in Kosai. Even that Nana Serwaa understood. Then he proceeds in Kosini for the benefit of the stranger. His matters are no reports that must be conceded from the stranger. On the contrary, they are a story, and a matter that involves the very stranger. But with the tale the wise man proceeds, as to entertain the table before the next and final matter of the night.

Negutu told the ancient tale of Mzizi, The Fortune of Misfortune. In that world famous tale, the character Mzizi lost both parents at sea, and found himself a slave in a strange country. Seeking always a run away in search of his land of nativity, he confided in a fellow slave, an older gentleman. Mzizi told of his kingdom, of his family and the richness, and then, finally, that he was heir to the throne. In fact, he was to be crowned king, now that his parents had died. But by some strange fate, the same by which he lost his parents, he was slave in an unknown kingdom. Said to him the old man, "there is no difference betwixt a slave and a prince. Of a truth, all is of the same substance. The outer manifestations are our confusions. In the case, my son, that you realize this, and know how that you can change your outer manifestation, again, I say, you can be a prince, or even a king. And should you perceive that the possibility is to go home to your country of nativity, I urge you to reflect on the very stories you have read me. Stories of men that became great in foreign countries. Never then, I say as a friend, think of home as the redemption from your condition; it's naught but an illusion. Of one we are all made – humans and animals and lands and the richness of the earth are of one. The mind, Mzizi, contains the will by which a man endures than a camel, and the resources by which he may create his estates." The story concludes with Mzizi becoming prince of the very land he was slave in, and then a king.

Tonight, sipping on his third cup of guna, he ended his tale. His listeners knew his tale was directed as a comfort to Nana Serwaa. And the poor soul could hear no better words and enjoy no better comfort than this inspiration. Yes, not mere comfort or palliative balm to the wound, but an inspiration to healing. Even Queen Kalima in her heart of hearts is thankful that a fellow woman taken into captivity can find some solace in Netugu's tale. Now, however, the wise man must proceed with the final matter on the night. And delicately so. For such a matter will draw from the depth of his wits.

The master of craft did not fail to impress his lord. For Nana Serwaa, he stated, it was a choice she had to make or not. That she was under no compulsion; and in the case that she did not consent to marrying King Buka, she would still be accorded a reasonable respect and will learn to become of some other use to the king's service. Nevertheless, she is encouraged – not mandated to accept the king's honor of an excursion about the kingdom. Turning to Queen Kalima, even more carefully, he deliberated the goods of the possibility of a second wife for the king. And as he spoke on, he moved his cup unto mid table as he could, without taking his eyes off Kalima, who sat on the left of the king – his far right. And the moment seemed magical, for the queen leaned forward, hoping as much to look at Negutu and be looked at. "Your Majesty, your father is one of the wisest men I have every encounter. His wisdom, I am certain, abides in his offspring. My counsellorship has always been easy because of the wisdom of our king, but I must confess it has been easier since the day of your arrival. Born a royal yourself, Your Majesty, the importance of a child cannot be overemphasized. These years without a royal seed has attracted some disquiet or anxiety, permit me say, in every level of the kingdom. But time has a way of succoring us when we expect it least." He turned his gaze to the king who nodded approvingly, almost careless of the queen's dropped face.

"There is this mystery I observed in my youth, and it holds true in my years of hoar hairs. Pregnancy, in a certain sense, is contagious. A pregnant woman is like a mirror to her fellow women around. For every time a maid conceived, betrothed or not, another closer to her also did. Whether it was fearing such a thing or wishing for it, I cannot safely say, but the effect is my concern, Your Majesties, ladies and gentlemen. A pregnant woman courts much attention and thus easily enters and can occupy the minds of family and friends. For us men, it is merely to care for the pregnant woman, whereas, for a woman, she imagines herself in such a state from time to time...Until it becomes her reality. If fortune be friendly toward our king, and the princess Nana Serwaa agrees to be his wife, I would that you take her as your sister, Your Majesty. For through her pregnancy, it may be, you will also bring forth children unto the king – your lord and husband. May the words of your servant be viewed in their truth" Emusheguta Negutu the Wise concluded, bowing his head first toward the king, then the queen.

"The queen may have a word," King Buka said, gesturing to the queen with a smile and a hand. And without addressing the table guests, she spoke right on in a manner quite simple and unusual of her: "Your Majesty the king, Emusheguta Negutu has spoken wisely, as is common of him. My part is to fall in line where Your Majesty and our guest should concur. And that I haply shall." The king nodded to Negutu, who knew what was next to do. Without much a say, he called to Nana Serwaa to speak as she found fit.

Nana Serwaa Berimah addressed the diners accordingly. Her manners were noticeably graceful and courtly, and so were her choice of words and gestures. But these men and women were unsurprised, knowing how much time and effort are absorbed in Akan courts on the subject. And Oman for nearly two centuries have been the epitome of Akan civilization. So this anxious table is all ears to hear the guest speak beyond pleasantries, the Wa-Zangan hospitality, and the royal house's graciousness among others Nana Serwaa is speaking about. But Nana Serwaa is also very shrewd. She is aware that however nice these people may be, they are her captors. If she cannot satisfy their request, she may not last in this foreign land. There may be no going home for her. So she thinks to herself first to buy time, for per adventure her husband will come and rescue her.

So she continues onto the big matter with eyes hardly directed at anyone in particular; not even the queen that sat directly opposite her. "Uh...Your Majesty is young and handsome, intelligent and gay-spirited, and kind hearted and generous." She bowed somewhat shyly to the queen, who with a nod and gesture of the eyes implored her on. It will be an honor to serve you as a wife. But now that your servant is distressed and is in much confusion over the state of her country and peoples, and forgive me add, the wellbeing of my husband, it is ill time that I should answer Your Majesty in earnest. Yet (she looks slowly around at everyone), if His Majesty permits, I shall need a little space of time – two or three moons, to part with my land of nativity and my kinsmen and husband, and embrace the destiny the gods have carved me. Finally, if your servant is any favorable in your eyes, and were it possible for you, I would know the fate of my husband – Nana Yaw Edusei, my father's house, Oman and all of our people brought here into captivity. I cannot ask more, Your Majesty King Buka. To you I am grateful, Your Majesty Queen Kalima. My heart reaches out to you Emusheguta Negutu for your words of wisdom, and for your graces I am much delighted, Honorable Generals, and you, My Ladies."

In the fewest words possible King Buka assured Nana Serwaa that she will have a full 3 moons to make a decision, reassuring her that she was under no compulsion to please the king with her decision. He also promised she will have all of the information required duly, and that Emusheguta Negutu will be the one to speak with her on every concern of now and that shall arise. Having thus spoken, the king thanked everyone for honoring him and the queen with their presences, and called the dinner over "Oumotu, kashi banquiti dka gmhune... Your presence has made for a great banquet. See you on the morrow." Of course, it was 'see you on the morrow' because Kosai made no room for good night. The night was not good according to tradition, because the sleeping man seldom had power over the wandering spirits that possessed the souls of men by night; people simply wished each other another day. And here we find where the French and now English borrowed word – banquet, must have come from; from the Kosai word banquiti which means a formal dining complimented with meeting or storytelling.

It was many years ago, sometime in the mid-1400s, when the Italian explorers Alvise Cadamosto and Antoniotto Usodimare visited the Malian Empire. Prominent among their associates journeying with them were three French Christian missionaries that took serious interest in trading, according to imperial counselor and historian Zhandaiki Gawo Aghi. Aghi's parchments have it that these French journeyed south after coming to Niani in the Malian Empire, where they parted company with Cadamosto and Usodimare. And they came down to Oadugu, capital of Wa-Zanga in its prime. There they encountered great civilization and wealth, and knowledge of the arts and medical sciences far above any people known to them at home and abroad. These missionaries were often at the king's court, and traded linen and cotton fabrics and kitchenware for gold. Many a night they were the king's guests at 'banquiti,' a term which Jean Paul Babin, one of the three missionary-merchants popularized in his 1458 kitchen classic *Cuisine des Africains*. The French also engaged scholars periodically, learned the imperial Kosai language, and traveled the kingdom, until a full year was done. Then they went back north to Niani and returned westward to board a vessel home.

CHAPTER III

O MAN WAS LARGELY PEACEFUL THROUGHOUT the reign of Nana Berimah. He built a wall around his kingdom with the three countries and kingdom that bordered Oman. By extending invitations to these neighbors to attend Omanian ceremonies and honoring their invitations and giving expensive gifts duly to them, Nana Berimah won over these rulers and their subjects into a compelling friendship and formidable alliance. But it became apparent to Oman's neighbors that the elite Akan kingdom was no longer interested in their friendship. The interim governor before Yaw Edusei had failed to honor various invitations from these neighbors, and worse, he organized the swearing in of the new governor – Yaw Edusei without an invitation to a neighbor, and the Governor Yaw had married Nana Serwaa, careless of their neighbors' attendance. Hence, when one of these neighbors was attacked, they sought peace where else than Oman. They did not send a word to Oman. Thus the little kingdom was totally taken by surprise at the attack of Buka and his men.

It is a week since the attack on Oman. Six days have come and gone by, and here is the seventh, since the queen and other citizens of Oman were taken captives. Each day leading up to this has seen consultations on consultations between officials of Oman and her neighbors from Kudi. The neighbor has been very instrumental with the intelligence on Buka and his kingdom available to Oman. But the attack tactics implored by Buka and his men, their maneuverings in transporting captives, their motive and inspiration, and the entrances to Wa-Zanga or the terrain and conditions will scarcely suffice in rescuing the captives by arms. Yaw Edusei has reasoned that, after varying proposals from his military commanders. Oman has diplomacy as her best option, but just how they go about it poses questions and inspires further cliquing, as with the pro military proposition.

Nana Yaw Edusei is wary making any enemy for himself among these people he is still largely a stranger to. To take to any of the three peaceful plans may jeopardize his friendship with members of the other two factions, and he may lose their loyalty. The earlier is technically insignificant, but the latter – the losing of loyalty he holds genuinely fundamental. So he lay in bed restless, with his mind entertaining a thousand thoughts about the new love of his life that was taken away like a bird broke out of his cage, the several citizens of Oman taken captive whose families come to his court every day to inquire of them, the council members, the future of the greater Ashanti Kingdom, and imperative as any, if not more, the matter of a child to call his own.

But Yaw is no fool. He is not sent over here to become governor merely because he is cousin and friend of the exiled Otumfuo Nana Prempeh I. Neither is his position predicated on sympathy felt toward him by the latter. Contrary to these already unaccepted presumptions and whatever may aid in the decision, it is largely due to Yaw's abilities as a soldier and a statesman. And such a man as he knows full well that thoughts must be entertained one at a time. For to awake unto the morrow without a decision on which proposition Oman would use to save the captives would not only prove his inability to rule, but bring into disrepute the astuteness of Otumfuo Prempeh I's decisions.

The man that came atop his class at the Wesleyan High School and went on again to achieve the highest honor at the Royal Ashanti Military Academy was quite aware of all that was at stake. Honor. Pride. Ashanti! As he pondered the key objects at stake, he reckoned what must be done. Slowly but meticulously he revisited each of the three prepositions mentally. He cautioned himself about objectivity over sympathy, about the best cause over the least best, irrespective of which powerbrokers stood aback of that preposition. No sooner had he played the prepositions in mind than realize they all bore strategies that required careful considerations. At that moment he decided that each had to be put on the table, but the top of each plan. Finally, he picked one strategy apiece from two prepositions, and two from the third. All of the accompanying trivial, or "seeming trivial" as Yaw would put it, will be easily left to his discretion by his officials.

Yaw went over the four again mentally: Oman would pay no ransom, since that would indicate weakness, and give Wa-Zanga the power to demand more; apparently more than they could offer, thereby losing any chance of winning back the captives. They will offer proposition of alliance between the two kingdoms; particularly, Oman will offer to support Buka and his kingdom whenever they were attacked, noting possible invader in Wa-Zanga's Boro neighbor to their northwest that constantly attacked them. And while they seek negotiations, they will in no way prepare for war, at least not until negotiation crashes or fails to meet their general expectation. Mention the great worth in gold and livestock that Buka plundered from their kingdom, but declare that, in good faith that shall be forged on a cordial agreement, the kingdom of Oman does not require them (Oman requires only her citizens and whoever among the captives was resident therein).

After going through them, Yaw hesitated. He perceived that there was scarcely any leverage for Oman, especially not in dealing with a ruthless raider that laid waste your land and took your wife and other citizens captive. But that was a start, he comforted himself. More critically at the moment is the delegation to pursue this undertaking on behalf of Oman. 5 officials crossed his mind. Then he dropped it, considering that that is too low a number. For, he reasoned, they are most likely to entertain a deviate thought; the fewer people are, the more likely they may agree on a matter. But many people will seldom find concord in a matter; the chance of an unlikely agreement between them increases the possibility of them delivering on the objective of their mission. Thus Yaw settled on 10 officials. And his mind continued to race and the governor would entertain no sleep. Who are the men to make the delegation? Cognizant of their cliquing and various factions, Yaw decided the delegation will comprise members of the 3 Omanian factions known to him, and members of his staff brought over from Kumasi. By morning he will inform the council of his decision, and liaise with them to field the delegation. To sleep he must retire for a couple hour respite. And into the hands of the gods he committed both great and small matters of his life and the kingdom.

He opened his eyes to the darkness of the room, heedless of the woman laying by his side. His eyes had been shut all those hours he spent finding solutions to the pressing matters of the state. He closes his eyes again, this time to sleep. But a strange thought flashed into his mind. Could somebody have already taken his wife as their woman? Is she sold into slavery? What will her master use her for? She was too beautiful and intelligent for any sensible slave master to waste in the field. If he were that master, he would take her as a wife. Yes, even with a hundred wives to his belt, he will not hesitate. What if she is sold and at a very high price which is the likelihood? Will he pay her price? What about the other 143 captives? Would he pay their price? Could he afford it?

But they are not personally his. They are the state's. Well, can the state afford the price of 143 captives? For he would pay the price, whatever it was in gold, for Nana Serwaa's freedom. He smiled, as the thought of whether it was freedom for her hit him. Even he knew that Nana Serwaa's marriage to him was an arrangement, which was possibly against her will. But that was the custom. The girls he was attracted to as a child have only lived in his memory. It was a base thing, a thing of ordinary peasants and merchants to choose their own spouses. But maybe, no, truly, he conceded, their subjects are free in that and they, the rulers, are the bondmen. Those and many other things did Yaw ponder relating to Nana Serwaa, before merciful sleep took hold of him. O momentary sleep, how sweet.

And all those hours Yaw Edusei laid on his bed, Nana Serwaa Berimah did same in a strange country. But while he had a bedmate, she slept solitarily. And she was content so, for why would she have one in this strange place. Her husband is home, hopefully. She craves his arms, and longs for his touch, as tears trickled sideways of her pearl eyes while she yearns to feel the warmth of his breath on her scalp – between her threaded locks. His figure so gigantic and yet his personality so gentle; he was the only man she has known, and she cannot imagine there is any better. Besides, her father had always told her that every woman has her own best man, and that is her husband. She had observed that her father was not fully right in that, but she was glad such was her personal experience.

All the nights since they were married, Nana Yaw Edusei entertained only her in the governor's chamber, the same that belonged to her parents. The very room in which her mother conceived her. There was not a night for her mate, who was useless in the eyes of Yaw, though he hated to think of her with any disgust. But he did not treat her any differently in private. And thought Nana Serwaa had pleaded with him to be kind to her, he always stated that there was not a problem. He just did not love her anymore, and yet he could not put her away. But Nana Serwaa knew better. Everyone knew. The Eduseis were unhappy because there was no child born into their marriage. But such unhappiness was not strange to her. She found that her own parents had wanted a boy in her stead, and though they loved her, they had prefer if she were a boy. As she reflected on that, a thought struck her that made her wonder. How long has she been married? How long does it take a woman to get pregnant? It is running to a year, Nana Serwaa Berimah. She is frightened by the thought. And several questions flooded her mind: Am I barren too? Was my lord already feeling unhappy about this situation? She could not think of a moment that suggested that, and so the questions continued. Is Yaw Edusie cursed? Is she or the Berimahs cursed? And with Ashanti's recent fate she questioned if Ashanti and anyone that had association with her was under a curse. Of course, her family's and Yaw's are just two of several cases among royal Asantes and their cousins or associates. Every following thought only increased fear and made the teen tremble from panic upon her bed.

As quickly as she managed, she switched her thoughts to the world she was now in. Wa-Zanga now held her fate. Whatever it was she could not be sure, and she was equally afraid of the possibilities as she has become of Oman and Ashanti and her husband this night. But tomorrow King Buka shows her his kingdom. His proposal to her is already official. And as much as she is uncomfortable with the thought, she has to face it she cautions herself. And now.

She began by thinking of Buka and all the good things she has noticed and heard about him. Indeed, she knew Buka was so handsome and so kind and so intelligent that he was almost irresistible to any woman including her. But only almost irresistible. For where is virtue, she thought as a warning. It is fair for every man to be handsome and kind and brilliant, but every woman needs just one. She has accepted one man into her life already. It is only a man that can have two women, not the reverse. But she achingly realized that Buka truly did not care. Not as long as he is the only man here in Wa-Zanga to call her his own. And she was certain she could not refuse his proposal. At least not for a long time. She could buy some time; it may be Yaw Edusei will come rescue her. Or could Yaw and Oman have abandoned her and the other captives to their fates? Poor soul, too many questions and scarcely any answer. Or answers you cannot find the strength to accept. Broken by her thoughts Nana Serwaa crashes into her tear-wetted bed.

The morning sun was bright as the eyes Nana Serwaa took courage to stare into. She had been riding along with Buka on his onyx black stallion. He had paid a somewhat fortune for two from an Arabian trader when he visited the Malian Empire a few years back. Nana Serwaa's inability to ride a horse had put the king at an advantage. She had sat in front of him as he took her sightseeing of his kingdom. He sat in a wild tumaki garden, a tropical flower that will safely pass for an orchid family. The tumakis were in rich purple and white, covering two thirds of an acre. A 6 square feet open wall tent housed the pair. Buka had just asked her if she loved her husband very much. Her heart seemed to stop within her, as she wondered a dozen things that might imply. But she braced herself, looked the king in the eyes, and answered most respectfully and yet truly: "yes, my lord, I love him so." The king, who looked down into the hard-staring eyes set in a face that bore both seriousness and yet a pleasantness, felt the vibration of the truth of her words. He was disappointed, but felt his love for her grow even stronger. He asked a question, a hard one, and She had only just given him the equivalent in answer.

He seated himself and invited her to sit, pointing at the chair to his left. A small tea table separated the two chairs that faced in the direction of the city. From that highland in the tumaki garden, a great part of the city, including the palace, was visible to them. He showed her various landmarks from their seats, and as he pointed out his palace, he saw her curiously twist and look toward him through his peripheral. Her mouth had half opened as if to speak, then she caught herself. But not early enough for Buka, who asked her to speak freely her mind.

It was nothing she could say, for how could even a teenage girl with no battle experience note the vulnerability of Wa-Wazanga, the king and his palace. And if that was an honest vulnerability, of what advantage was it to discuss with the man who has brought her captive out of her country. The Omanian army could attack Wa-Zanga from this eastern hills she thought. But how would they know? Who would betray Buka to her? And if one were willing, what price could she offer, being a captive and with no purse in a foreign land. But this must be the will of the gods, she decided. And who was she to fight against the gods? They were nobler in their dealings than humankind, and if she thought otherwise, they were still the gods. They fashioned everything – good and evil, as they would, and human's course was to walk or be led accordingly. Such a hard thing to grasp. Even the priests were so limited in their understanding of the gods. So, till the gods make known their will, it is an honorable thing to work and fight and devise to one's benefit; such is the wise thing to do, and to fold our hands and wait on the god or the priest, the foolish. Nana Serwaa, after rationalizing thus, told King Buka faintly, "your servant is only amazed at the splendor of your kingdom." The king nodded and motioned to her. It was time to get back to the palace. Then, looking away from her and struggling how to address her he said "remember, your ---- ladyship, at noon you will be the guest of Emusheguta Negutu. You will have a carriage and maid to escort there."

Yaw Edusei awoke strong. His cold bath concluded the magic. Each time he had a demanding day coming up, he took the problems to bed, allowed his (conscious) mind to work to solve them, and so strongly hypnotized himself with the matter that his sub conscious mind went to work on it while he slept. And when he awakes, he spends a full hour in the bathroom, mostly running cold water bath. The cold water refreshes him and opens his mind and he can quickly think up solutions to problems he was faced with the night before. This was a lesson taught him and other members of his class at the Ashanti Royal Military Academy (ARMA), and something he has put to work many times and successfully.

On such mornings, Yaw's custom was to have only tea for breakfast. And he loved these meetings as early as possible. He was the first man in the conference room, and it was nothing short of strange. He would enter the conference room ahead of meeting schedule, sit in his seat, and play out the meeting mentally. He could be sure of the sitting positions of certain council members, and those were the ones he gave voices to and proceeded to discuss the matters on hand. Within 12 minutes he could see the discussion at a near conclusion, after which he summoned and informed his aid to allow council men into the conference room once they arrived for the meeting.

The meeting got underway by 9:00AM. There were 9 members in attendance, beside the Queen Mother and Governor. For the best part of the meeting, it was information presented to the council by the governor. He informed them of his decision to utilize four strategies from the three prepositions presented him by the council. Then he moved to discuss the delegation, allowing for input from the council. He had intended to make conference as brief as feasible. The presented the council more of decisions virtually nothing requiring deliberations, safe for the delegation members. But even that he simplified somewhat by giving three council men the task of appointing two people each to the delegation. Two members of the Berimah family will be selected to the delegation by the Queen Mother of Oman, the mother of Nana Serwaa. Yaw Edusei had conceived this thought in the bathroom a few hours earlier. And finally, on the delegation, two members of his staff from Kumasi will be a part. Yaw had already decided on the men of his staffing. They had served with him sincerely and diligently while he was in the Otumfuo service, and he brought them here to Oman on this assignment because he could trust them.

The meeting concluded with the date on which to dispatch the delegation. Everyone tasked with presenting delegate will submit their picks to the governor by the morrow. The hour and venue are unchanged. Provisions will be made for the trip, and gift for the king of Wa-Zanga readied. Oman will pay no ransom, but even the governor reasoned with the Queen Mother that one cannot leave from a distant country and go before a foreign king without gift. Civility demanded it, and Oman, though settled on not paying ransom, will present a golden dove to the king of Wa-Zanga. The golden dove symbolizes the peaceful nature of the delegates' quest. The Royal Treasurer will now get to work on these tasks and see off the delegation in three days.

At noon, a palace attendant called on Nana Serwaa who was already dressed for lunch with Negutu. Promptly she availed herself. A maiden was earlier introduced to her. Djaimara was the maid's name. She would attend to Nana Serwaa for as long as she was the king's guest. She walked outside with the Lady – Nana Serwaa, as they were led to a human-carriage. The carriage was planted on two long poles that rested on the shoulders of four men – a pair each back and front of the cabin. It seated two people. The young women got in and the men – bondmen from faraway lands, raised the poles onto their shoulders with the cabin, and followed the palace attendant who led them to the counselor's residence. The day was hot, a temperature of over 95 degrees. While the women were comforted by rich Arabian fabrics that dressed the carriage interior including its roof, the four men carrying them had only enough to cover their male sexual organs. But their butts were exposed, and so were their thighs downwards, and entire upper parts from their waists.

It was 18 minutes over to the counselor's residence. The men had one break which was a fifty count by the palace attendant. That is an approximated one minute. When they arrived at Negutu's residence, sweat dripped from the men profusely. They were visibly exhausted. Nana Serwaa was deeply troubled at this sight. She gazed at her maid a couple times to perceive what she thought of the slave men, but the young girl seemed careless of the carriers. And so did the attendant, except that he had to control them for the safety and expediency of the Lady Nana Serwaa that was in his care.

"The High Counselor of Wa-Zanga!" shouted the attendant with a bow, as the ladies stepped out of the carriage and just outside the porch of Negutu who was standing at the entrance to receive his guest. The maid bowed as the attendant, while Nana Serwaa bowed slightly but slowly in reverence of the elderly noble. The nobleman returned his guest's bow and ushered her in. They took seats on the porch for as few minutes where they exchanged pleasantries, before Negutu announced it was time for lunch. He gestured to Nana Serwaa who followed him into the hall and through it to the dining room. It was commonplace for Negutu's children to eat lunch and dinner with their father. But today they are forbidden from lunch. The wise man knows too well that though his two sons are unmarried, even they may take interest in the Omanian youth and thereby embarrass him with the king. He hated to entertain it, but endangerment, and not embarrassment would be the case if any of his sons were to take interest in Nana Serwaa. The pair has a 6 feet table stretched out with delicacies, of which Ostrich is the delicacy of the day.

There were a dozen meals – appetizers, soups, roasts, and bread and rice and ducor. There was ostrich meat in soups, roasted, as well as the egg scramble-cooked. Negutu urged his guest to get down to eating. There was so much to eat as there was to talk about. But now was eating time. As for talk, Emusheguta and his lord King Buka had it all planned. The news of the captives was in their sole power, and for a fact they have kept them well. Of Oman, they have concocted a grave story. They will fabricate another version of the Oman attack, in which they will declare the governor's death. Negutu had a brilliant account of how the events transpired and how they came to know the governor had died. He was a man revered for his cleverness, but not vices. Yet today, at the king's request, he must do the unwanted. It was an order, not a request, and the wise man knew full well. He had seen four kings in this kingdom, and has served three. And the first rule that has kept him alive to date and prospered him is obedience. Unconditional obedience.

They quickly left from appetizer to main courses. Nana Serwaa took servings of ostrich egg and the ogun sauce. The servant was happy to have the stranger try out the ostrich egg. Ostrich was a priced delicacy here because it was rare, except at the table of the rulers. They loved it and would have it as often as they would, especially when there were guests to show off before. Even Negutu could not miss the opportunity. He was incredibly delighted to hear his guest confess that she had never had the bird for meal before. It did not matter much that culture and not status of affluence could have kept the young lady from eating ostrich in her kingdom. He was simply elated to have introduced her to the esteemed delicacy. Nana Serwaa took her first piece without dipping it into the sauce in order to ascertain the taste of the egg. But sadly, it went bad for her. Before she reached a second piece into her mouth from the sauce, she was choking. Negutu's female servant who served lunch quickly reached over with a napkin and led the guest out of the dining room.

Nana Serwaa vomited the egg and much more. The elderly woman was alarmed. It was no common response to ostrich egg. She suspected the young girl was pregnant. And before they had left the private room where she cared for Nana Serwaa, a nurse was in. Even Negutu suspected the young girl must be pregnant and therefore sent for a nurse instead of a doctor. The nurse examined Nana Serwaa and found her to be pregnant and with a slight fever and considerably high level of stress. She returned to the hall to give the Counselor her findings.

Emusheguta Negutu was anxious and nervous and confused. Today has certainly been like no other day in his decades of services to the throne. But he reckoned it was another problem as any other he has encountered in his counsellorship, only that its name and subjects may be different. That was Negutu's solace. And from that consolation he moved chonological steps to settle his anxiety and nervousness and confusion. Firstly, he reaffirmed that the practitioner was good at her vocation and had settled the question; the Omanian was pregnant. Second, the king, by the gods will understand that the situation with Nana Serwaa was an unforeseen mishap; they could have done nothing about it. Thirdly and finally, his lord will appreciate that he had said nothing of their machination before the girl fell ill. Only one thing remains certain, he concluded mentally: Buka will have a doctor check Nana Serwaa without his knowledge. The king trusted nobody, and he conceded his distrust carefully. But Negutu had served him too long to be oblivious of the fact. He hoped, again, that the nurse was right. At the least, that whichever doctor the king requested to check Nana Serwaa would confirm the diagnosis reported by the nurse.

Nana Serwaa, as confirmed by the king's physician, is pregnant, stressed and feverish. The diagnosis brought joy to Nana Serwaa, who believed that with this pregnancy, she would escape the net of the king. At least it should buy her enough time for Oman and her husband to intervene and save them. But again, she reflected on a question she had considered during the past night: could Yaw and Oman have abandoned her and the other captives to their fates? She could believe in no answer; not a yes or no. Only the gods knew, and that they have hid from her. She can only hope by some chance she returns to the land of her ancestors again.

But until such a time, Wa-Zanga – her present reality demands much of her. It asks questions that she must answer, or rather, the answers she must accept to live with. To live, not merely for herself anymore, but for her unborn. So the young girl takes satisfaction in her pregnancy, in spite the circumstances of the time.

But her head captor is disappointed. Buka had got the news while at lunch with the queen. He refused to continue with his meal. He has foregone his dinner too. The capture of Nana Serwaa presented him a new hope. Hope of a son. Confidence of an heir of his loins. The captive from Oman was a foreigner, but so was the queen. The law of inheritance applied to the subjects of the throne, not the throne. This he knew, and was bracing himself to take a second wife. It was in his interest, his forefathers, and the kingdom's. Even more, she was not from Wa-Zanga, for such a wife he was reluctant to take. But with Nana Serwaa's pregnancy, his hope is dashed. As much as Buka hated to think that the gods controlled the events of humankind, today, he has thought, the gods were most unkind to him. How could they give him so much hope and then crush them right in his breast before they are established? But as the question settled in, he realized, as always, he could not rely on the gods. They were no friends of man. He had to work out the course of his life and both object and means were his to determine. The fate of the foolish and weak is in the hands of the gods, but the wise and mighty man carves out his own path. By morning he will consult Negutu on the matter.

CHAPTER IV

K ING BUKA IS UP EARLY as always, but today much more early. He slept with the night and awoke with the morning. It was binding on humanity, and the king even more. Many men had a life of their own, but the king lives more for the kingdom, and less for himself. To say the least, he lives to the principles and traditions to which he is guardian. Oh, he thought, the king is scarcely anything more than that. But there is no place and time for philosophizing, he cautions himself. He has matters of the continuity of the Kuhu dynasty at hand. Emotion can have no place now. He will depend on his intellect and have reason triumph over sentiment. So the king prepares himself, and eats breakfast while his counselor Negutu is summoned.

Emusheguta Negutu spent the night equally worried, or rather, in great thoughts about the pregnancy of the captive girl. He knew he will be advising the king on the matter the next day. Certainly by morning. He would call on the king if the latter did not request his presence. So the old man walked through a dozen thoughts, including possible decision to make on the pregnancy situation. His grandfather use to say that the thoughts of a thousand people may be less powerful than a concentrated thought of a single man, but if converted and applied into his purpose, such power is so great that everything is possible to achieve. A quick marriage between the king and the royal captive would lead Wa-Zanga to believe she was carrying the king's child. Peradventure it may be a girl, and Nana Serwaa could go right on from there to give the king childfren from his own loins. Wa-Zanga would put its faith in the marriage and children will be born unto the king. If the pregnancy now results in a male child, the succession matter will be settled based on the fact known to him and the king. But now they must use the energy of the kingdom to the advantage of the king.

Nana Serwaa was served breakfast in her room at the king's order. Unsure why, but he had directed the palace steward to keep a nurse always in the Lady Serwaa's chamber, and that her assigned maid should be the only one to serve her food. Also, a guard was to stand post at the door of her chambers. The queen had servants and two guards posted at the entry to her chambers. The guards changed shift every 4 hours. In the strongest terms the king cautioned the Palace Steward to ensure no guard served more than one chamber. She is not to leave her chamber until the king had ordered otherwise. But it was the direct order to Nana Serwaa, which came the moment the physician had pronounced her diagnosis, that made her panicked and confused: to speak to no one about her pregnancy or any matter relating to Oman. Technically, the king had prevented her from speaking to anybody. Every servant that served or had direct contact with her was under such directive. And what was there, of Wa-Zanga, for the poor captive to talk about. She was only a stranger. If she says or asks a hard thing, her servants will refrain from speaking. She was silenced, in a great sense, but for what she knows not.

Wa-Zanga's High Counselor arrived at the palace as quick as he could. His valet was used to preparing him at such impromptu summons. His master was an important figure in the kingdom and closest confidant of the king. There hardly was a decision passed in the kingdom which Negutu had no knowledge of. In fact, too many were his workings than the king. With the events of yesterday, both he and his valet anticipated the summon. Together with his master Negutu, they were too experienced in official matters and knew the king too well to be wrong. And so he got the old man up shortly after the break of dawn, and readied him for another critical day. And here, Emusheguta Negutu presents himself before his lord - king Buka, who sat unusually alone in the hall of his chamber. Not unusual in times of vital decision making, the old counselor realized.

As the guard stepped out and closed the door, the king called out to his counselor "Emusheguta!" Trice he did mention the name and with such power that one may safely assume for both excitement and the summoning of courage. As he called out, he left his seat and helped the old man settle into a chair as he routinely did. Negutu was not so old, or rather not so weak to say the least. But he enjoyed this habit of the young and energetic king. He was the chief strategist and propagator of the continuation of the Kuhu dynasty after the demise of Suka, the king's father. And ever since Buka became king, he has been grateful to the great counselor. He has held Negutu in a fatherly place, and the old man has not failed to impress accordingly.

When both men were seated, their eyes made a moment's contact: in the king's eyes were questions the old man understand, whilst in the old man's eyes was light that indicated to the king, all is well. But just how well could this be? He has not known the young woman intimately and the child could never be his. Why is Negutu courageous? Has the sage of Wa-Zanga discovered reason for esperance? Buka could hold his patience no more or keep his mind wandering into the sea of the High Counselor's mind. Is not Negutu present and will speak at my request? So the king broke the silence, asking the kingdom's oldest serving official, "what is responsible for this light in your eyes, Emusheguta Negutu? Of a truth you must have stumbled on a fortune I know not of." Before he had paused, he realized 'stumble' was not the word. The man who at age 27 counseled his grandfather, and served his father in similar capacity, Buka recognizes, is a master strategist. He creates every piece of what becomes a plan. Stumbling was for student, but the creating was for masters. And his counselor, indeed, is a master strategist.

Emusheguta Negutu is revered as a counselor because of his pragmatism. For over four decades he built a repetition for giving counsels that are doable. He was a philosopher, but also a very clever man who gives the simplest practical steps to executing his every plan. Today, he advises the king to take Nana Serwaa as his wife in no later than 7 days. The king was away from home for 35 days, and the Lady Serwaa rode with the king after the sorting of the captives through to Wa-Zanga. And here at home, of course, the king has had private occasions with the young girl. The queen will assume one thing: the king must have already had an affair with the royal captive. The People of Wa-Zanga will believe whatever information presented them. The possibility was strong. But what about the woman herself? Of course, she knows the one that impregnated her, yet she is the king's subject and will do according as he commanded. For the sake of herself and the unborn and the women and children here in captivity she will obey the king's directives.

After the first child is born, the king can have as many children as he would with her. We can hope that this pregnancy is a girl. Otherwise, we can only hope for another boy that will be truly of Wa-Zanga. If such a one is born, some mishap will befall the elder son which is now conceived. And the king shall have a son of his loins to sit on his throne when he crosses over to his ancestors.

"There is a swifter measure, my lord, to the matter at hand. But I did not advise this, because I have learned by experience the gravity of catastrophe a possible accident poses. A physician may terminate the pregnancy immediately, but if something goes amiss, this woman I see you already love will be of no use to you other than a bedmate. And if she be reduced to such, of what advantage is she than the queen" Negutu cautioned, almost biting his lips with the latter statement. Then he proceeded "therefore have your servant resorted to that which may seem an elongated course, but which, I say, is secure and feasible."

There was a single gap or important possibility almost left out by the High Counselor that Buka noticed. And he had given the king counsel on what should be done. But to the king's amazement, the old sage of Wa-Zanga touched that possibility – the abortion measure, before he had made an end of speaking. Negutu has never ceased to dumbfound his lord. As if he knew that that was on the king's mind. Whatever, it was an option he had weighed but it was found deficient. Emusheguta completed his deliberation to a not-so-surprised applause from King Buka. And with that the old man is certain that such and such will meet the king's decision.

But just how to proceed with it required discussion between the two. The details leading up to the marriage may seem small, but they are complex and critical. So the men were locked in for two hours overall. Negutu will visit Nana Serwaa in her chambers before he leaves the palace. The Lady will be free to go out, as well as speak to anybody. Including the queen. But her security will remain intact. In fact, two guards will now stand post at her chamber doors. The men have noted that such a matter is likely to displease the queen. She may become bitter, but both men agreed that the queen would show no rage. And therein lay the danger: A silent enemy is worse than an outspoken one.

9:06AM, Oman

The members of the delegation were present along with the councilmen, the Queen Mother, and the Governor. Yaw Edusei sat in the ruler's seat, as always, and was seated a full hour before the attendants were ushered in and seated. The Governor had spent a near fifteen minutes with the Queen Mother, after which the councilmen and the delegates were called in. Everything has gone according to plan, the Governor's aide, who met with every council member and delegates, informed the assembly. He had taken account of all the delegates including the Governor's and Queen Mother's picks. Also, he met with the Royal Treasurer who is here present, and assures the assembly that the propositions of the discussions of yesterday met with great success. The Royal Treasurer also gives details of the assembly's requirements for the delegates traveling to Wa-Zanga. The governor now moves the meeting to introduction of delegates.

The process started with councilmen introducing their delegate picks. The introduction comprised name, family, rank or station, and a feat that distinguished the individual from an ordinary man, in order to determine his pedigree and ability. This would enable the assembly to choose a spokesperson, a deputy, a counselor, a captain, and an administrator. The Queen Mother took over from the councilmen to introduce her picks, and after her the Governor took center stage and followed suit.

Of especial note were three gentlemen. The first, a pick of the Queen Mother, was the spokesperson and voice of her late husband in his latter days. He was a cousin of Nana Serwaa and had the business of advising King Berimah on evolving scientific and explorative events including trade and colonization that were reshaping the political and geographical realities of man and his region. He learned at the feet of Renaissance Muhammad Al Hunti, the legendary scholarly from Alexandria, who sat at the feet of Rifa'a el-Tahtawi, the pioneer of the Arabic Nahda. Many Omanians had wanted the young man to become king or ruler after Nana Berimah. They believed that with his knowledge, Oman will become stronger and independent of Ashanti. But sadly, he was not a Berimah. Even more, the young man had no inclination to serve as king; his sole interest had been in improving the life of his people through education of modern government and the arts and sciences.

The second gentleman, presented by a councilman, was popularly known as Tuoza. The 50 year old was at a point in his life the second most respectable man in all of Oman, second to the king Nana Berimah himself. He had no blood ties to the throne, neither a connection through marriage. He became administrator of the small kingdom due to his ingenuity. He had no more than 5 years of schooling, but for 20 years recorded various events and projects and day to day task as administrator. He was very instrumental in avoiding a fight and possible overthrow by Ashanti in the past two decades. By understanding the great power of Ashanti and the shortfalls in Oman's strength, he talked boldly with the king on the matter and approached the Ashanti throne in Kumasi at each time a new ruler assumed the throne in Kumasi. And he negotiated an annual tribute which was nothing too great for Oman to offer in exchange for an ideal level of independence.

Over five years before the passing of Nana Berimah, the man lost his wife in an unprecedented circumstances. To alcohol he resorted to find comfort, and forgo his duties to the throne. For a fact, he was of no use to the king's service. But shortly before his demise, the king requested his presence in the palace. He showed up a shame and disgrace for an Omanian, the ruler observed. But this was a man that had advised the king and has been a citizen of immense repute in the kingdom. Perhaps he could return an advice Nana Berimah thought. And that he did, prompting his former administrator to make him a promise to abstain from alcohol. Ever since, Tuoza quitted drinking, and has realized that his sanity is especially needed now that his master is dead.

In 1890, when the pepper and palm crisis confronted the Ashanti Kingdom, it required an expedition to Liberia. Nana Yaw Edusei led that expedition. His first deputy lost his life in what is today's Ivory Coast. And so did his deputy replacement. Then it fell to a young soldier, who was a product of the Ashanti Royal

54

Military Academy. He was only 20 years old when the expedition kicked off. The day Yaw Edusei made him his deputy was the same day on which the soldier turned 21. And, it was on this same day that he saved Yaw's life in the same attack that took the second deputy's. From that moment onward, as Yaw's career has progressed, so has the fortune of that soldier. Today he is Yaw's chief aide, and best trusted soldier and most loyal friend. His name is Kofi Gyasi.

The three men, Nana Kwasi Bosompem, Tuoza, and Kofi Gyasi will serve as Spokesperson, Administrator, and Captain respectively of the mission to Wa-Zanga. Tuoza, who is also fluent in Kosini, will be deputy speaker. The captain and the pair are to be present in every meeting. For once Nana Kwasi will have to leave the side of his master because he is the only person among Yaw's aides from Kumasi that spoke Kosini. So he will be the governor's eye. But not anyone was to know he spoke or understood Kosini. Not until the necessity outweighed the conceding thereof. Everyone knows he will be Yaw's eyes on this diplomatic mission, but at least not any one Omanian knows he speaks both Kosini and Kosai.

Every delegate making the journey was assigned a specific task. Their allowance was decided. On the morning before they departed – in two days, they will hold a brief meeting with the governor. The council will also meet and brief him on the progress of the trip the night before. Finally, the delegates will pick up the golden dove during their final meeting.

The council expected it will be two more days before the delegation departed for Wa-Zanga. But that was not to be. During the night, the delegation secretly converged at the palace. The treasurer had delivered the provisions and allowances. He also delivered the golden dove – the present to King Buka. All of the men will sleep in the palace and depart Oman at first light.

Yaw Edusei was the governor. But he was not merely a diplomat or statesman; he was a militant. He was also trained in intelligence at ARMA. There was limit to his trust. And with too many people involved in the meetings for the diplomatic mission, he will take no chance. The governor will need all his wits to count in the matter at hand. The lives of hundreds of his people are involved. Even more, the life of the princess Oman, his love, is at stake. The attack on Oman for Yaw, must have an inside hand. What strangers could know the place so well and the ideal time to attack?

He will later inform the council that he had to see the men off earlier due to the delicateness of the circumstances. Yaw, of course does not expect the council will receive the information warmly. But as much as a cordial relationship with the council is important for his governing, the success of the trip is even more so. A broken relationship with the council may sure be mended if the Wa-Zanga mission is successful. But to keep the council fully involved in the process at the possible expense of a compromised trip due to leaked information will come at a priceless cost. He will fail all his life to restitute for the loss of the Omanian citizens. Some may term his decision emotional, subject to his affection for Nana Serwaa and free of any held obligation to the other Omanian captives. He will call it a hard decision of empirical reason over official cordiality. Whatever is said, the end will justify whom it will, and condemn the unjustified. Indisputably, it is a way of life, and that Nana Yaw Edusei, Governor of Oman, acknowledges.

By 4:30AM the delegates met with the governor one final time. The first person up was Kofi Gyasi. His commander and governor speaks with him a final time in private before the meeting in the governor's living room. Yaw seeks to use the occasion to make a final case of the mission for which these

selected few will feel motivated to undertake, and inspired to give their all. He will use the common denominators between the delegates to state his commissioning of them:

"Great men, you may be Omanians and Asantes embarking on this great mission, but be reminded that you are all Akan. One mother and father gave birth to you. By the blood we share, which binds us closer than the geography and culture and many simple things that divide us, we are bound to a common destiny: unity and dominance, prosperity and endurance of the Akan tribes. Our disunity prevents us, but to recognize our common identity is to thrive in our every quest. Past Ashanti kings have destroyed kingdoms around and exacted great tributes from many, but Ashanti has never been to war with Oman. And Oman has paid only a fragment compared with other lords in the regions about Ashanti; and those kingdoms are not half free as Oman.

And if I may again remind you: whatever your occupations, vocations and estates, you are all soldiers. A soldier once, a soldier always. I cannot overstate the soldier's duty, and yet I will not delay you by speaking of it, because you know it as much as I do.

So today, as you go on your journey, go on in the Akan spirit. The gods of our ancestors carry you, be with you, and bring you back with success."

Wa-Zanga

Today is the second day since Nana Serwaa fell sick. The day before, the High Counselor met with her in her chambers. He informed her of the king's decisions. She is free to leave the palace and visit the locations in the city and may take excursions to the countryside provided it is arranged timely. Negutu notified her of the number of surviving captives from her country, and the king's decision to have at least 5 of them visit her daily. An allowance will be provided her periodically, as well as new garments bought her from the merchants who will bring their wares on display at her chamber. As many garments and jewelries as she may desire, the royal coffers will cover. Her allowances is to be used for charity and the rare things a lady may buy for herself. The young girl listened to the old man with a heart so grateful to the king that she was eager to cut him off and speak of the gratitude that so filled her heart. But she was mindful to be patient, for a lady had to keep her manners tactfully above her emotions.

Negutu told of all the king's orders, gifts and promises. Then he got to the one thing that will alarm the poor girl or distress her soul. And of that he was mindful, but he was obligated to deliver his master's message. Even more, he had to do it as best as possible. So he told Nana Serwaa about Buka's decision to marry her no later than two weeks. The sooner they have preparations underway, a date may be established. He looked to her a moment and turned away. For he could not look longer at the happy-turned-gloomy figure with cast down face that sat across from him. How long he has been engaged in such work, and yet Emusheguta Negutu has never found it easy to deliver hard news. His son would tell him that it was the king's words, and not his. But his heart has been cut many times by such messages, and his only consolation has been that it was also his duty – a sworn obligation to his master, to undertake faithfully. And every time, his conscience pricks him. Not merely because of the possible victim of his message, but because he felt his execution of such tasks fell short of faithfulness.

The High Counselor had made an end of speaking a whole minute, and there was no word from the royal captive. Negutu looked toward her, hoping she will catch his look and say something. But she did not lift her head, neither said a word. What was there to be said? The words of the king were decisions, and his subjects had to accept and yield to such conclusions. It did not have to please them; their happiness or wishes were only worthy of daylight if they were parallel to their master's. Even she was a subject of Buka and had to do according as he bade her. Whatever she suffers or enjoys will be at the king's pleasure. To reject the king is to suffer what she and her unborn and her people here in captivity may not survive. And to accept him is beneficial for all of them, and yet even more, for the buying of time. For what king will touch a woman impregnated by another man? Of course, not Buka, she thought. Consequently she raised her head, with a somewhat cheerful face and a smile she attempted to conceal.

"Emusheguta, it is no trivial a matter that weights on me. And all, yes all is known to you and the king. I am the wife of another man, and that is a vow I would wish to keep. But if it pleases the king to have me as a wife, and the gods have so apportioned me such a fate, who am I? Our lord the king is a good man. That my people and I have found grace in his sight, it is even more beholden of me to honor him unconditionally." She bowed her head, and as she lifted it and Negutu thinking she was done speaking, she continued "You will tell the king his servant may be despaired at some times, but she joyfully accepts to be his wife."

Old Negutu was happy there was good news for the king. But of course he did not agree she was happy; he simply perceived, with all of the stakes in her reality, she was merely content. He trusted however that Buka will so fill her world in a short while that her husband will fade off of her memory. The High Counselor left her chamber with a visibly bright smile.

Just a day later, Nana Serwaa is smiling, as she lay in her bed after her bath. Breakfast is ready, but she is complacent to indulge herself in the well of thoughts that bring smile to her face that has become accustomed to grim. She agreed it was all the will of the gods. The will of the gods is done in the life of the righteous and unrighteous alike. It is up to humans to plan out their life, but it is the gods that determine the destiny of every creature. And the gods must have determined such and such fate for her. To accept the will of the god was a path of peace, but to reject was misery and failing – a person swimming contrary and perpetually to the flow of a river.

Just as the thoughts made her smile and she chuckled, she caught herself. Was she unrighteous? Why would the gods allow her to carry the child of one man and marry another? Could such a way of the gods be just for the righteous? Perhaps, it may be a punishment for her unrighteousness. And though she could not perceive her wrong doings or sins, she simply accepts that people may stray from the right paths in ways they know not. For how else could she reconcile the judgment of the gods who are just and nothing less?

When the High Counselor left her chamber yesterday's afternoon, she promised herself one thing: to live out each day happily as possible. Her heart was resolute to accept the will of the gods. For, she ponders, they do know the future of all minds and all things, whereas we know only that which is already happened. With that mindset and a cheerful countenance, Nana Serwaa got out of bed and dressed up for breakfast.

In the middle of her breakfast, Nana Serwaa received an unexpected guest. It was the queen. She had heard of the captive girl's illness and upcoming marriage to the king. Kalima had therefore called on her to express her to express her congratulations for both the stranger's pregnancy and proposed marriage. The queen handled the gifts from her maid before entering. She bore them herself and presented to the woman who is soon to give her husband a child. Queen Kalima's gifts included fruits and a robe she got as a gift from her father. It was never worn, and now she offers it to the stranger. There was hardly any better gift to demonstrate her affection for Nana Serwaa, and that is something anyone may observe.

The young girl received the gifts from the queen and put them away appropriately. Nobody was to present her food besides her maid servant assigned to her chamber. But this was the queen; such law did not imply to her. Or so did Nana Serwaa perceived. And all her staff. She put the fruit away simply because it was ill-custom to eat food or open present before the presenter. She will definitely eat it when the queen departs her chamber.

Before she left her, Queen Kalima informed Nana Serwaa that she will do everything in her power to support her wedding to the king. And she will intercede with the king for the welfare of her countrymen. She asked only one thing of the perplexed girl who stared at her with obvious confusion. And that the young girl promised the queen. So Kalima left knowing she could count on the word – the integrity of a fellow royal and woman.

The maid servant and nurse rushed to the room. Shaking, the maid asked Nana Serwaa if she had eaten anything from the queen. Of course not. The maid was alarmed, and so the nurse. There was no former grounds on which to distrust the queen. But the circumstances involving the girl and the king and the queen were ground enough. A woman could be easily aroused to jealousy over her fellow who carries the child of her husband, especially if she was unfortunate give him one. The case is no strange with Queen Kalima. They two servants therefore advised the trashing of the fruits. It will be their responsibility, the maid particularly, if anything went wrong with the king's bride in waiting. But think all they may, Kalima was too ingenious to make such a move. That would have been an act of desperation, a cheap emotion the queen is incredibly wary of.

The queen was informed of Nana Serwaa's ailment and her to-be-marriage with the king the past evening. She decided during the night to pay the girl a visit. She thought hard for the best present she could offer her informal mate. The robe stood out, and when she was done with breakfast this morning, she called on the Lady. For a fact, Kalima has already held a first meeting with her staff to plan for the wedding, which date is unknown, except that it is shortly. Many of them expressed sadness about the matter, but the queen was not the kind to allow somebody to pity her. She never pitied herself, and she will allow nobody the prospect. She is strong and practical, virtuous and generous. That has been the woman she has shown her staff and the kingdom at large.

But Kalima had had no occasion to exhibit any contrary act. Her husband had been hers, and hers truly. In spite his frustrations at her apparent barrenness, he treated her lovingly and respectfully. It was not always easy, but that she understood. He is human and susceptible to frustration. But the queen was capable of everything devious. And only one person – her head maid, knew that here in Wa-Zanga. And so when Kalima had her staff meeting, her head maid knew there was more to these talks. Kalima came a long way here with her help. Her help may again be required by the queen.

CHAPTER V

FIVE DAYS LATER, THE ANNOUNCEMENT of the king's wedding was publicized in the kingdom. Various preparations were underway, including the king and Nana Serwaa's personal preparations. There will be no foreign invitation. The wedding will be nowhere as glamorous as the king and the queen's. But it is the king getting marry, however again, and the groundworks must prove befitting. The wedding will mark a new birth of hope for an heir to the throne, and many of the people, in spite their love for the queen, welcome the new bride.

The mojo in the Great Hall at Wa-Zanga is awesome since the wedding announcement a day ago. Various officials and prominent citizens have called on the king. A few of them were given audience with the bride. They brought in gifts for the king and the bride. A few brought in gifts for the gracious queen, who has accepted the wedding. They could not suppose she was glad, neither did they consider it was based on her acceptance. It was mere courtesy to suggest that Queen Kalima was gracious and accepted the marriage of her husband to another woman. It was the king's decision and that everyone knew. The words and presents to the queen were simply formality to say the least.

But just before Noon, a delegation was announced in the king's ears as he sat with guests in the Great Hall. Buka's cheerful facial expression dropped like a mask off his face. He dismissed the guests and sent for his chief counselor and army commander. He requested that no one, including the Queen and Nana Serwaa was to enter the Hall until he ordered otherwise. His concern was Nana Serwaa, but he was mindful lest she become alarmed.

Off to his chamber he went. He will first consult with his officials who are expected shortly.

The king and the two officials entered the hall after their somewhat brief meeting. Present were ten men from Oman. Their spokesman is the young Nana Kwasi Bosompem, who introduced himself and all of his fellows to the king and his officials. Afterwards, he took seat accordingly. The king's counselor took turn to formally introduce the king, himself and the army chief to the delegation. When he had so proceeded, he entreated of the men their purpose of call. And swiftly but carefully the speaker of the 10 presented a gift before the throne, which the army commander reached for and received on behalf of the king. Then the speaker – Nana Kwasi Bosompem returned and stood before his seat and spoke:

"Your Majesty, the Royal High Counselor, the Royal Army Commander, and the peoples of Wa-Zanga, we have come in peace. The gods of our fathers do us worse, than they already have orchestrated against us in recent times, if we have otherwise visited your peacefully laying kingdom.

Of a fact, in a war between our peoples, even most recently, if your Majesty may allow his servant freely speak..." he gestured with his head to King Buka for approval, but the king's face was stern and unfriendly. So the young man quickly jumped from speaking of anything that may seem to incriminate or could possibly offend the man sitting on the throne. But there was no word that would not offend. There was nothing that could be said without casting of blame or accusing Wa-Zanga of wrong. It was almost impossible, or rather bluntly, impossible for the young man. And as it became increasingly clear to the young Bosempem, he looked to his aged deputy Tuoza, who had perceived the difficulty the young man was faced with and had informed himself it was a probable thing to approach Buka with Oman's plea and not upset the king.

The Omanian sat in a row across from Buka's officials. The king's throne was at the head of the room, with his officials on his right and the visitors on his left. Tuoza got up slowly from his seat as he motioned to the young man to sit. His slow movement was in reverence to the king and as a security precaution, rather than age or the feebleness of his knees. For, unlike the former speaker Nana Kwasi Bosompem who stood up before his seat to address the king of Wa-Zanga, the older speaker had moved to the middle and bowed himself with a knee to the floor. As he lifted his head, he saw the king motion warmly to him to stand up. It was the first sign of friendship or warmth from Buka within these 15 minutes gone. And that was rightly interpreted by the wise Tuoza, who proceeded to address the king. He started off with pleasantries and then went on to the pressing matters at hand.

"Your Majesty King Buka, Oman will take pleasure in your friendship. You are a great king, and our people have acknowledged that we were too conceited to keep friendship with our immediate neighbors and forgo that with kingdoms far and abroad. We are bound by no law that prohibits any one kingdom from attacking the other. Allies may be bound to pledges and conventions, but there is nothing of such that obligates us one to another. We therefore do not judge it wrong to have been attacked by Wa-Zanga, neither the taking into captivity of our peoples, of which, notably, is our princess.

"But, your Majesty, you will agree with your servant that Oman cannot disparage ourselves further. The consequences of our past way of diplomacy is enough lesson, and from that we have moved forward and are come, and do now call on you – Your Majesty King Buka and the people of Wa-Zanga, in friendship that should bind us and our posterity to generations. Yes, indeed, we seek friendship.

"Moreover, your servant will make a more audacious request, but nothing too great that transcends your noble and lofty generosity. Humbly, every citizen of Oman including the governor, Nana Yaw Edusei, beseech your kindness in setting free the Omanian captives of the war of yesterday. All of our leaders recognize that war is present where alliance is absent. It is our hope that on this ground we – Oman and Wa-Zanga will forge an eternal friendship. And for our part, because of this priceless debt we shall bear toward you for the release of the captives, we pledge an unconditional alliance subject to no convention or agreement Oman is presently bound by, and should ever be, in the future that stretches endlessly ahead. Your Majesty, honorable royal officials, we are grateful for your friendly welcome, and more so for your ears," Tuoza concluded, bowing his entire upper half before retiring to his seat.

Buka was moved, and so were Negutu and the commander. They were even more in a fix, because it was difficult for the king to speak on any of the matters proposed by Tuoza without conceding. It was too early to say the least. So he gave Negutu the hand, trusting the wise counselor will speak accordingly without making any concession; not in this first meeting. And Negutu spoke lengthily, telling of Wa-Zanga's honor and culture and civilization, and the latter he stressed as if to dispel any possible preconception the men may hold against Wa-Zangan civilization. For the counselor was not ignorant that the image of the kingdom was a disgrace in foreign kingdoms and lands; but to a larger extent he knew those notions were fallacies. He concluded with a promise of Wa-Zangan hospitality as he assured them the king will speak on the Omanian proposals duly. In the meanwhile, he encouraged the delegation to feel at home as Wa-Zanga hosts them tonight.

The Omanian delegation left the Great Hall in high spirits, grateful to the former administrator. Years of excessive drinking seemed to have no effect on his brain. His brain, but not his body. At 50 Tuoza was somewhat too frail for an Omanian man. Yet some may argue that most men of Oman had served in the military, and so they prided in their physical appearance. But Tuoza spent his own years of military training and service in learning. In the presence of the gods, as the Omanians would say of him. For what man could know so much of near and distant countries, having never left his native Oman, or schooled past second grade. For all his schoolings were in the 5 years a Libyan scholar stayed and educated young boys in basic reading and writing in Oman. So short a time for anyone to be versed in English and French and Philosophy and Mathematics. In fact, Tuoza set up a system of accounting by which Oman's expenditures and incomes were listed and calculated, providing the king periodically with a clear status of the royal economy. The man advised Nana Berimah on everything from politics to trade. And in spite his non-physical features, he was found to be a brilliant military strategist. The late king would joke that the gods gave him body fit to sit on the throne, and Tuoza's brains to keep it. And indeed, for many years, that proved true.

As the three men sat alone in the Great Hall, the king asked his officials for their impressions, if any. Of course, they knew, Buka never accepted a 'no opinion.' One could not listen and understand without forming an opinion. Each man will speak his mind, beginning with the commander.

The army chief indicated that the long term survival of Wa-Zanga will be determined by the potency of its alliances. The many small kingdoms and chiefdoms and lands in the region and about are carful of the future, especially now that foreign peoples and faraway lords are seeking to take control of new territories and expand their kingdoms respectively. The one lord and kingdom that can bring many into a league will not only protect his kingdom, but expand his power. Now that Ashanti's power is broken by the British, its peoples and allies are in need of a protector. As a unit Wa-Zanga may seem insignificant, but with many such kingdoms that fear the fate of Ashanti and other kingdoms, King Buka can lead a new world order that restores hopes and grants peace and protection to the peoples. With Oman as an ally, Wa-Zanga can rally many more allies that a broken Ashanti empire has left neglected.

The commander spoke, apparently careless of the circumstances the king is faced with. His reasoning was sound, the king acknowledged, but reckoned also that his commander did not put all the cards on the table. At least Nana Serwaa was missing. Yes, coalition is important, but what about the image of the king. He has announced to the kingdom his coming marriage of a second wife. No sooner had his announcement gone about Wa-Zanga than the coming of the Omanian delegation with a proposition that will terminate not just Buka's marriage, but his hope of an heir. And his commander did not cogitate a balance of the both critical demands facing Wa-Zanga, but restricted his deliberations merely to foreign politics. The king tried hard not to show his disappointment. But it was obvious for someone that knew Buka well, and the man reflected suddenly and felt ashamed of himself. And this was no time to go over and make amends. He will find another way to appease his master. Now they will hear from Negutu.

Emusheguta Negutu was not a god, and that King Buka knew. But the old man walked in the wisdom of the gods. He was almost faultless in his counsels of three generations of Wa-Zangan kings. And Buka has loved him most, apparently because Negutu has become wiser with the years through experience. And today, like many times before, the stakes are high. The king is stressed and is not in the best state of mind to choose pure reasons void of emotional relief. At least a dose of emotional relief will serve as balm on this wound the gods themselves must have inflicted on him. But even that seems unlikely now. Negutu, like himself, is only human; though men claim of them both to bear the spirits of the gods.

"No one can explain or truly understand the melodies of your heart, as it pertains to the Lady Serwaa, my lord. But we may empathize with you because we have been in love at some time in our lives, too." As he said that, Negutu realized that the commander is still in love. It is he who has lost a love to death. But of course he is still in love with her memories. "Your Majesty is wise and knows the sheer difference between wisdom and sympathy. It is unfit to pity the king, because it is ill for anyone to perceive ill of you. I will therefore speak of time and chance and the fable that ordinary men say of them.

"Time and chance, the mundane of humankind, teach their fellows to take full advantage thereof. They say that when chance avails itself, one cannot postpone the time. Opportunity does not come twice. That concludes their philosophy of life. But I will point out by experience that such is indeed the viewpoint of banal men and the birth place of rash decisions that lead to irreversible fatality."

The counselor went on with examples of people that saw seeming opportunities for opportunities and did not investigate, thereby taking advantage of it and falling into some catastrophe by the very decision they took. He admitted his wrong in advising the king in the Nana Serwaa matter. He implored the king also to see that fate is on their side, when these Omanians show up before they executed the plan of marriage. Certainly, it is a difficult thing to send out a cancellation of marriage announcement, but it is the better option than continuing. There are many advantages for the king and the kingdom with putting so great a debt on the head of Oman. It will be an eternal debt Wa-Zanga can use to its great advantage. And it will pave the way for the massive alliance mentioned. Oh, and needless mention that in these alliances the most beautiful daughters of kingdoms far and near will be Buka's to have. The king may love again than he has never before. For great men are able to love stronger than the former (though Negutu did not love again; he never sought to. Besides, years were not any friendly to the aging counselor). And sons and daughters will be born to the king.

"Your majesty, we may be of no help to you right now. It may appear we are careless of your dilemma, but we do care. And though you may go to bed tonight with much confusion and a cast down spirit, we know you and do trust that when the new day comes, you will awake as the lion – Buka!" the old man ended speaking, drawing a short but rather surprised laugh from the king.

Buka stood up with a warm smile on his face, reached out to his officials and shook each of them heartily but without a word, and retired to his room. The men sat for a moment wondering. Then the commander broke the silence, asking "Emusheguta, what do you think?" But the counselor only smiled and motioned to his comrade that they should take their leave of the palace. The aged counselor had had enough this afternoon. So much depended on him than his comrade royal official. Besides, Negutu had cautioned himself that he was a civilian and his comrade was a militant. In spite his conviction that the commander was a noble man, he trusted no one, especially not a militant. He had seen trusted advisors put to the death, and by the hands of such men. He is fearless of death, and that Negutu likes to remind himself, but to the grave he seeks to go honorably.

During the night, King Buka called on Nana Serwaa in her chambers. Her attendants were all dismissed, providing for a private meeting between the two. Buka had spent hours in bed pondering the request of the Omanian delegation and the advice of his counselors. Whatever the many words of each of the officials was, they meant one thing, and that Buka understood:

Let the captives (Nana Serwaa) in particular go. It had occurred to Buka that his officials were careless of the other captives, but he reckoned as well that they were insignificant. To let them all go would scarcely cost him loss, but Nana Serwaa is priceless. He was in love with her. He will not let her go, at least not without a try or fight.

Tonight he sits next to her, deliberately seeking to touch her body, to feel the warm body of the pregnant. He dares to know if it is the warm temperature of her fever that will exude from her, or love within her breast that answers to his. Or, perhaps, if it is the coldness of hate, or the almost undetermined temperature of confusion. The king, with all his wits, was sadly certain of the latter.

"Princess Serwaa" Buka calls softly and calculatingly to the captive. He is determined to speak a few words as possible. And he will leave without seeking to hear from the girl, for he wishes not that she should speak forth any word out of duress. In fact, he has come to let the bird loose from its cage. "It is my natural right to be in love with whom I may, as much as it is yours to accept or fall in love with whom your heart pleases. I love you, and my heart breaks by the mere thought of losing you. No, it is this rather: my heart is crushed within me because I cannot have you to wife. I have resolved to let you go, because it is uncouth to have a woman against her will; it is no different from a fowler trapping and encaging a happy flying bird. No amount of care can prevent it from falling sick; the sky is its delight. I am today the fowler, and you are that bird. I set you free."

Nana Serwaa cannot control her tears, as they flooded from her eyes down her cheeks. Her body suddenly quivered. Buka hesitates, then leans sideway and takes her head into his chest and wraps his arms and hands around her. There is a long pause of words. Then Nana Serwaa is stable and breaks the silence "My Lord..." But Buka admonishes that she needs not say a word. "Don't." He paused, weighing his following words. "There is a delegation here from Oman. They beseech my release of every

Omanian captive. It appears they came in peace, and are honest about their petitions. The old man Tuoza has the spirit of the gods in him; but even he did not persuade me to let go of you and your people. I am rather persuaded by your love and commitment to your husband, to put it lightly. Put extremely, but yet earnestly, I am persuaded by your rejection of my love and proposal; I reckon that they fail to meet your heart's approval.

"You may leave on the morrow or whichever date you find fit. Your nurse and maid may accompany you, to ensure your safety and that of the unborn. Provision will be made for you and your people's return." Slowly, he unwrapped her from his arms, sat her upright, and knelt before her. It dawned on her that this was not merely the king of Wa-Zanga speaking to her, but a man deeply in love with her. She saw the fire – passion, truth and love in the brown eyes that stared right into hers. Her heart skipped a beat and broke in confusion. She could not be sure of what she felt toward this man. And if she loved him, how possible. She was in love with her husband. At least that she entertained void of the slightest doubt and free of any reservation. But if her heart could accommodate love for two men, what did it matter? The life of a moral woman can contain only a man at a time. And Yaw was present, in spite of the physical reality of his absence. For, it was only a matter of time before she returns to him. So what is there to offer Buka? Neither sympathy nor empathy availed much to ease the pain of his broken heart, his longing soul and restless spirit. Not even a word of any sort. And so she falls back in her seat – sank deeper into her confusion, oblivious of the king and her space about her.

"May the gods lead you safely to the land of your fathers, and be with you. But if it be their will, that fortune forsakes you in the very country of your nativity, you may freely return. My doors are opened to you, eternally." With those words the king stood up and left the Lady Serwaa's chamber. Nana Serwaa was certain that Buka's words were true - that he meant, more than Wa-Zanga, the doors of his heart. So she closed her eyes tightly, dreading the thought. A return to Wa-Zanga is a most unlikely option, and to let loose of her bond to Yaw Edusei is even unthinkable! These and several other thoughts engulfed the poor captive, but as it crossed her mind that all things are in accordance as the gods will, she collapsed. The will of the gods are ever unknown to man, and worse, they are often strange; who can comprehend?

The delegation could not wait to know the king's decision. Their night was long and filled with questions, and the morning has not come with answers. At least nothing is told them of the king's decision. Not even the queen or the High Counselor is aware of Buka's decision. If it pleases the lord of Wa-Zanga, he will speak with them. For all certainty, if Buka himself sends for them, the news is largely a good one. If it is a rejection of their petition, an official is the most likely person to deliver the news. This is a rationale shared by the majority of these men. As they eat breakfast this morning in the guest house where they are lodged, their great hope is to have an ordinary attendant come in, rather than a high ranking official which might likely be informing them of some dreaded decision of the king.

In the palace, Nana Serwaa awoke late. Her nurse practically slept in her bed, monitoring the sick princess the night through. Her mind is still in a state of grave confusion that her body fails to process any clear emotion. Her temperature is normal, the nurse noted. But the princess did not appear to want to talk. And the experienced practitioner was careful not to speak or ask amiss, lest she trigger an emotion that sends the girl into a worse state. So the woman let the Lady Serwaa be. She will speak when she can.

In his chamber, King Buka had sent for the Royal Treasurer, the Royal Army Commander, and the Royal High Counselor. They are meeting over breakfast. The king enquired of the latter two if they had any reservation about their counsels of last night. Both men hesitated, choked on speech, and nodded disapprovingly. The king addressed the pair by their titles, and informed them that their counsel is upheld. The commander and counselor could not hide their satisfaction at the king's words. This decision, they are convinced, will go a long way for the peace, security, prosperity and longevity of the kingdom. They bowed in reverence to the king, who motioned to them to sit. "You resisted the natural inclination of counselors to appease the king, and truly counseled me in the right way. I am indebted to you for your courage and sincerity. This generous kingdom will reward you duly, for it never disregards the noble services of its citizens.

Every captive of Oman will be presented to the Omanian officials here who will lead their people home with escort from the royal army. Let them be provided for adequately and appropriately, according to the munificence and vast treasure of Wa-Zanga. I will personally acquaint the delegation with my decision, after which they shall have access to their citizens, including the princess.

The preservation of the kingdom and possible expansion of our power rely greatly on foreign diplomacy and skillful political and military maneuvering. An integration force made up of kingdoms that will share our ordeals will be irresistible, and we can lead a new world of kingdoms wherein every king maintains a great level of sovereignty. Every king or lord wants to continue his rule. To devise a means by which their lands are protected and their wealth is increased, we will bind them in a confederacy that Wa-Zanga leads. And to that they will gladly obligate themselves." The king paused, look in the direction of his high counselor, and smiled.

"Emusheguta, you are a man of great wisdom. The speaker of the Omanian delegation – the aged man Tuoza...extend him an invitation for lunch. He may be of great advantage to this objective. And I trust that you will find a way to secure his friendship. It is in no way a betrayal of his master, therefore I am convinced you will prevail with him, and shortly we will have the great plan set."

The king went on to discuss dinner for their guests. Oman had already pledged to align itself with Wa-Zanga. Therefore they will have the Omanians take the stage and inform the king of possible ways Wa-Zanga could help secure Oman and its neighbors against impending British occupation. The men of Oman will inform their insight of the region and prospect of alliances. However, the king and his officials are wary of Ashanti involvement. They will conceal their reservation from the Omanians, while they devise means to obligate Ashanti to a confederacy led by Wa-Zanga.

CHAPTER VI

T HE CAPTIVES LEAVE WA-ZANGA TOMORROW, save for Nana
Serwaa. She travels back home to Oman today. Escorting her
are three members of the Omanian delegation, and 15 men of
Buka's royal army. Also riding with her are the servant and nurse
that had attended her since her pregnancy diagnosis. One of the
three Omanian delegates escorting her was Kofi Gyasi. According
as Buka had promised, there was provision in abundance for the
princess' return, as well as the captives following her on the
morrow. Everyone that knew the king could vouch this one thing
of him: Buka is a man of his word.

The men walked at the front, and back and sideways of the
carriage in which were Nana Serwaa and her maid and nurse.
The carriage was driven by the royal expert driver and pulled
by two stallions. It was a rare thing to see the carriage anywhere
within Wa-Zanga recently. Queen Kalima was the only who rode
in it lately, but even that is years ago. She seldom goes out now
that Wa-Zanga is not so warm toward her due to her inability
to give the kingdom an heir. And before her, it was King Suka,
Buka's father that rode in a carriage nearly every place he went.
But not Buka. He thinks it is fit only for a woman to ride in a
carriage. Now, it is the princess of Oman that sits in a carriage
and rides through the city. Many wave at the carriage, unsure
of who is riding within. But if they were certain of one thing, it
is that somebody else, and not the king, was being escorted by
the royal army. And Nana Serwaa made it even difficult for the
people of Wa-Zanga as she kept the curtains closed. But now is
not the time for sentimentalism. She has to conserve her energy

for the journey she embarks on and the life that lays ahead for her in Oman. To greet and be greeted only raise questions, and such questions she wishes never to confront, especially now that she puts Wa-Zanga behind her with a return home.

Oman. The beautiful blue sky and lake. The hills and woods and getaways. The kind smiling people that never tire to greet. The Queen Mother – her mom. Her sisters and relatives. There could not be the like of Oman, a place so warm and beautiful. Oh, Nana Serwaa reminds herself that her youth is no more. She could no longer play with her cousins and friends before she was taken into captivity. It would continue same because she is still a wife, and especially now that she is with child. But she could enjoy those places with Yaw Edusei. But that is only if so much politics did not lay its weight on the governor. Be what may, Oman is home. There is only one home, and the gods sure appointed Oman, the happy returnee encouraged herself. Then she fell asleep.

King Buka holds a light reception for the Omanian delegates. They had feasted hard the night before. Tonight it must be simple, because tomorrow they will take charge of leading the captives back home. His guests have found him a most generous king and one to have as a friend. The king's top officials are present. Buka made sure of that. He was keen to impress the Omanians with his plan for a common league that protected all of the kingdoms signatory to its treaties. The men could not be less interested. For, if Ashanti could be subdued by the British, it is evident that a grand coalition of several states and kingdoms will be required to prevent British or any foreign occupation. Moreover, such an alliance will protect each ally from the other. This is the most definite path to safety.

As they wined and dined, Negutu made a final approach of Tuoza. Carefully as he could, he made conclusions to his plans which he presented Tuoza during lunch yesterday. Officials will be appointed to the league's council, and Tuoza is promised an office. It is an office that puts him in the running of the league, and in the interim, he will lobby with kingdoms neighboring Oman, and other Akan and sister states. He will appeal to each Ashanti chiefdom with the message of liberation. Ashanti will not take it easy to have a strange people or kingdom lead them in anything, but if it meant Ashanti restoration or liberation from British occupation, they are likely to welcome and comply with such proposition. And though the idea is pitched primarily to Tuoza, all of his comrade delegates are partially informed and are enthusiastic about it. Safe one delegate – Kofi Gyasi, Nana Yaw Edusei's deputy. He is the sole reason circumstances were artificially created and allowed for Nana Serwaa's departure a day before the rest of the Omanian captives.

The night before, the men drank heavily. Omanians and Wa-Zangans alike. Except for Buka, who drank moderately, because he trusted no one with his life, and Tuoza, who consumed no alcoholic beverage because of his dreaded past with it. Tonight, however, for the most part, the men are conferring about the welfare, and future protection and prosperity of their kingdoms. They have all forged a friendship over these few days, and rather unexpectedly. Obviously, so much achieved in so short a time.

Nana Serwaa and her escort have spent a first day and night on their journey. This second day is not so fair, for the sunshine intermits slowly on the partly clouded sky. But in spite the weather or whatever it threatens, one of this company of 20 remains joyful. It is Nana Serwaa. A return home means so much than any rain or shine can dictate. Her hope is kindled, joy is full, and will be made fuller when she steps her feet in Oman, the land of her conception. To have a husband move to live in her kingdom was a gift. Therefore, Oman is the one home she has known. And perhaps, the only home she will ever know.

An hour before daylight sprang forth, the second and final Omanian badge left Wa-Zanga. Tuoza took charge of leading the captives home to Oman, as he did with the delegation to Wa-Zanga. The man was loved and respected at home. And now, the gods have given him fame in Wa-Zanga. Talks of his wisdom soon rushed out of the palace into the commonplaces of Wa-Zanga, and the city had hoped to set their sight on a man carrying the spirit of the gods. Wa-Zanga had Negutu, but they could not resist to see the stranger. Buka and his counsel knowing the intention of their citizens, decided on the Omanians leaving that early. And though neither Buka nor Negutu took offense to the situation, they were careful not to permit a scene they could not fully predict. Especially because they will work with Tuoza in the formation of the Great League, and the execution of its goals.

On the third day of the journey it was as fair and warm as the first. Nana Serwaa had breakfast with her maid and nurse. The Wa-Zangan troop accompanying the Omanians ate together, and the three Omanian took delegates were a party. That was the meal setting since they embarked on this journey. Hardly anything unusual. And one a while, during breaks, the Omanian delegates including the leader Kofi Gyasi, spent time with the princess in conversation. She asked questions about home, craving to have this journey on with and to reunite with her husband and family and friends.

The sun is scorching this afternoon. The road runs through a thick forest, and travels through and by several kingdoms and countries. Sometime after midday, as they traveled past Indemba and come near to Osin, a strange twist of fate occurrs.

Nana Serwaa's train comes under attack. Everyone in the train is armed with gun, save the three women. As the ambush lays on the left and right sides of the road, the leader Kofi Gyasi urges the train to "speed ahead! No turning to the left or right. Everybody run straight ahead! Speed!" But before they had sped a near quarter miles from their attackers, and turned back to face them, two of their men were down. The leader got his troop in shooting positions on the road, while two men, including the driver, were to speed away with the carriage, and a second two were sent into the left and right sides of the bushes to inform the main company in case the attackers considered a bypass through the bushes.

Kofi Gyasi is young but considerably experienced, yet he is leading this train for a few important reasons. He is Yaw Edusei's right hand, for one, and even more importantly is the fact that the delegates had to have one of its members disguised, and therefore have him play no prominent part in the entire negotiations. But according to the contingency arranged, if such a thing as a battle started, the man is to take charge. And here, the leader asks that delegate to take charge.

The disguised Kwame Boakye, with only a nodding of the head, took charge. His first command was to fire sporadically as they could, while making a daring charge at the attackers. He was certain they were quite too few for their enemies. But a courageous charge, the veteran soldier is certain, may force the foes away into flight. For to escape was a near impossible task if the men insisted on pursuing them; and moving against this enemy is both daring and dangerous. Yet, to do neither of the two was to surrender to strangers they had not the slightest knowledge of. None could anticipate rightly that their lives would be spared. So this charge against the attackers, more than anything, is a most probable action. It is audacious, but they are courageous; it is a matter of life and death, but they are fearless. Duty to the princess supersedes their lives, and what is the excellence of a man's life, safe a noble end. If they should live, they would with the princess, and if they should die, for her they gladly will.

As the Omanians and their Wa-Zangan counterparts charged forward, their attackers withdrew slowly. But not for long. The enemy was certain it was only a matter of time before the defenders were out of armor. Moreover, as they withdrew, they split into three groups. The one stayed on the road and engaged the opponents, while the other two went into the forests on the left and right sides of the road, all with the intent of encircling the defenders. But time will not permit for such a plan, as the Omanian-Wazangan troop fell too fast. With only three of them standing, Kwame Boakye decided it was time to surrender. By his sides were two Wa-Zangan men, while Kofi Gyasi laid on the ground critically wounded. With two men on watches and two by his sides, it was apparent he could fight no more and his chance of escape was improbable. He signaled to his men, dropped his riffle, ripped his top covering garment and waved it in the air. The two men by his side followed suit.

To Kwame Boakye's utmost surprise their attackers dealt with them respectfully. The two men on watches in the bushes were called out. Their arms were taken from them, but they were neither tied nor molested. A very short man of just over 5ft appeared to be the commander. He issued instruction in a strange language, and all the men with him followed him on with haste, while 25 stayed to guide the 5 surrendered.

Obviously they are going after the princess, the venerable warrior thought. He grappled in the midst of this circumstance for an answer to the attack on them. Is it spontaneous? Or is it a design? Affirmative to the latter only suggests additional questions and answers, most of which this soldier could not answer or reasonably convince himself of. And though he failed to logically convince himself about his suspicions, in his heart he was confident Ashanti or Wa-Zanga had a hand in it. But Kwame Boakye is aware he made this trip because of his soldiery, not general wisdom; he accepts his limitations and embraces his strengths. The life of the princess is at stake, and that is the only concern worthy of contemplation. He redirects his focus where it ought, as he and the four Wa-Zangan walk in the midst of their captors.

Not quite 30 minutes had gone by, and the commander of the strange arm band met up with his team that escorted the 5 captives. Nana Serwaa had been captured, and the veteran Omanian soldier, engulfed in confusion of emotion, could only look on apathetically. As he was summoned to the front of the procession, he came face to face with the princess of his land of nativity; the very one he failed to save and that was taken into exile by Buka; now, she will be taken by a strange people whose tongue and appearance he still struggles to recognize. Kwame Boakye, for all his fame, had unsuccessfully protected the one true Omanian leader – Nana Serwaa. A second chance availed itself, and he has flopped.

With his head dropped in embarrassment, many sharp thoughts struck Kwame Boakye. The Omanians sing a song to his fame, and it has been sung for a generation. Girls and boys over 5 years sing his name and fame. But would cease after here, the warrior slaps himself with the hard fact. The end of one's life says it all. If that be any true, this man will go down in Omanian history as a failure and every word synonymous with disappointment. His youthful glory – wars won for Oman, the beating of the British while fighting for Ashanti, and his escaped in the Final Ashanti-British war, will go into oblivion. He will be remembered as the commander that lost the princess twice to barbarian arm men. The people of Oman will put that most callously; their sense of disgust and gratification toward a person are measured symmetrically. Oman has a place that hammocks on the shoulders of its citizens from generation to generation, for those that have done her service. Conversely, this elite Akan tribe has no place but a mire of their spit for the men and women that have let her down. The latter is where they will place Kwame Boakye and his memories, for failing to save the princess these two occasions.

The Omanian delegates led its citizens home anxiously. The women and children returning from captivity are even more anxious to reunite with their families. On this second day of their journey, they felt closer to home. It nears a second full day since they saw Wa-Zangan guards keeping eyes on them, safe a few who are now only protecting them as they journey homeward. As the sun set and they came down a hill and rounded a curve somewhere out of Dokum, a voice called out to them stop. The call was from behind. Anything from behind was dreaded by these traveling women and children, and their leaders no less. Looking behind for them was as terrifying as it was for the ecclesiastical escapees from Sodom and Gomora. A return to Wa-Zanga is unthinkable. However, they can breathe a mixture of relief as well as terror. It is Kwame Boakye, one of the delegates escorting the princess. He escaped after the capture, and spent the night and today walking in through bushes and coming onto the main road occasionally to meet up with the second train of returnees, and inform them of the tragic attack on his train and the subsequent capture of the princess.

Kwame Boakye takes the Omanian delegates aside and speaks with them. The men that attacked him and his fellows and captured the princess were from Indemba. But he cannot fathom why Indemba will be interested in the princess. He spoke rapidly, but softly and carefully. He was mindful of the Wa-Zangan escorts, as well as careful not to disturb the women with the news of the princess. But it was a useless attempt, for it was obvious to even the children. Before he was done speaking with his fellow delegates, the women had broken into lamentations:

Before her birth, Oman was excited

Then it was said that "a girl child is born"
And young and old wept for the royal house
Yet, sooner than later, the star shone bright
The hope, and the future of the kingdom
But the gods saw it fit to take her into captivity,
And with her the daughters and children of Oman
In this strange land Oman's star did shine
And through her the captive house of Oman did prosper
Then, when we had thought to call the strange land home
The gods forbade us, and out we are ushered,
Free as birds
But the light of Oman, where is she?

The delegates concluded their caucus. There were various opinions shared by delegates. Tuoza, however, had none to share. He could not make up his mind if the princess was the sole target, and who could possibly have been behind the attack. He simply told his comrades they were in no position, predicate on the information given by Kwame Boakye, to make a meaningful conclusion. Moreover, he was careful to not offend the strangers – the Wa-Zangans escorting them. So he moved over and addressed the train. Of the princess' capture he admitted, but intimated that they would get home safely. The incidence involving the princess, whatever accounts for it, is unique to the princess, Tuoza thought. He is certain to lead these men and women home safely.

Avoiding Indemba, and therefore Osin, puts them a day's journey back. On the eight day, as the sun goes past the middle of the horizon, the Omanian train, led by Tuoza, approached Oman. They were couple hours away from home, and eager to go on walking rather than rest in neighboring Kudi. But Tuoza insisted they rest, while he sent messengers ahead to inform the governor of their return and of the capture of Nana Serwaa.

Oman had to prepare for the return of its citizens. But more than that, the former admistration was careful not to arrive in Oman, have the people jubilate for the return of their families, friends, anx lovers, before they should learn of the Princess' fate. Today, he knew, would be worse for the kingdom than the death of King Berimah. The confusion of joy and sadness cuts deeper than the aches of loss. The Governor will be broken. The Queen Mother may not make it through. And Oman will sink deeper in the shadow waters of gloom. Tuoza cannot do more than afford Oman a few hours' notice to prepare for the news. At least, he hopes that suffices.

The messengers arrived in Oman and the news bearer was given audience with the governor promptly. The bearer give details of everything, putting the Princess' capture at the very end. Yaw Edusei shouted a great cry that seemed to be one of war and yet anguish. His soul crushed within, his heart was broke, and his mind ceased to function. He blacked out and fell from his seat.

The Governor's scream reverberated through the palace. The Queen Mother is alarmed and rushes to Yaw's quarters to inquire if all is well. She meets the messengers in the hall and inquired of the men, on oath of their lives, to inform her of her daughter. "On oath..." the Queen Mother insisted. A man under oath of the gods could speak no lie, except he wanted to die. For, in Oman, a person sick and suffering unbearable pains could speak a lie under oath or some ill against the gods, which, in anger, would slay the person. The men fell on their knees before the old woman, battered themselves by the gloomy news they bore, and teared up. They uttered no word, but this action prompted the poor woman to ask "is Nana Serwaa dead?" And to that one of the men jumped to his feet and informed the Queen Mother otherwise, explaining the circumstances of her daughter. But he is still speaking, and the Queen Mother falls off. The messenger on the ground, the one standing and delivering the news, and several others in the hall rushed to lend their arms. Arms, though, they lend in vain. For, today, Nana Ama Bosomtwe, Queen Mother of Oman and mother of Nana Serwaa, has just left to be with her ancestors and deceased husband Nana Berimah.

Nearing sunset, the returnees, led by Tuoza who is accompanied by the other delegates, arrive at home in Oman. Their arrival is met with mourning and whaling, not singing and dancing. Nana Serwaa is again taken, the Queen Mother is no more; Yaw Edusei is broken, and the future of Oman is unsure.

Tonight the kingdom will stay awake. The drummers and singers will lead all of its citizens through the mourning procession. But tonight will be unlike no other they have experienced, like none in Oman's history. They know, for the Queen Mother they must mourn. Yet, for Nana Serwaa, they are uncertain. Not even the officials of the kingdom can advise. So the singers and drummers will follow on as circumstances dictate. They cannot sing a song of hope, except hope reuniting in the afterlife. But what about Nana Serwaa? Is she dead? Must they hold no faith of her return? To these and many other questions the answers are unknown, or beyond the faith of these battered people. Only the gods can answer, but they do not speak anymore. No, not in Oman.

The escort guards of the second Omanian train returned safely home without anything dramatic. King Buka welcomed the men from his throne in the great hall. In persons were the Royal High Counselor, the Royal Army Commander and Treasurer. The guards reported of the safe arrival of the Omanians, and presented a gift of gratitude from them to Buka. But tonight in the Great Hall, everyone is paralyzed in their seats and speechless, when the news of Nana Serwaa's train is reported. For over a minute, not a word was said, neither a head lifted, nor an eye rolled in another direction. The room was dead, until the king broke the silence, asking his officials to go to their homes and rest. They will converge on the matter at lunchtime tomorrow. Everybody is dismissed.

The head guard from the escort to Oman returned to the palace later to give King Buka a letter from Tuoza. The Omanian requested that the letter be given to the king privately, and the guard did exactly that. The letter was written on a parchment in Kosai:

Your Majesty King Buka:

With highest gratitude I write to you. Your exceeding great kindness toward me and my people will be immortalized in the archives of Oman. But, my lord, I must inform you that the gods have wrecked a most terrible havoc on the people with whom is your best chance of leading the Great League. Nana Serwaa was taken captive by men from Indemba after her convoy was attacked. The Queen Mother, her mom, fell dead hearing the news.

The revival of a potential ally in Oman will, without an iota of doubt, be the return of Nana Serwaa. As glad as I had been, were the princess to arrive home accordingly, I am optimistic there can be no better time as now. Though her mother is dead, her return to Oman very shortly will revive this dead kingdom and spark a new fire to the torch in the hands of its leaders. Now, the power is in your hand to gain Oman's unflinching support in your ideals of the Great League.

My lord, the gods associate themselves with the cause of the mighty, but turn their backs on the flinching of men. The gods are with you, therefore, come now, I beseech you, to the aid of ally Oman.

Unpretentiously,

Your humblest servant

Tuoza

King Buka made an urgent summon of his army commander, treasurer and high counselor. Also in summon was the royal scribe. The king indicated to the men his intentions of going to war with Indemba, if they refuse, on his request, to release the princess Serwaa to him. His officials listened, and when he had made an end of speaking and asked for opinions, his high counselor rose from his seat and formally bowed before his lord.

"Your Majesty, in as much as I agree that having Nana Serwaa freed and delivered to her country is the wise thing to do, I would that Oman is involved. Call on them to avail men for this cause, as we would, and we can then make a siege about Indemba and demand what we may. I am convinced that even the head of their chief will be given us if we so demand. But to independently pursue this cause may have Oman perceiving a conspiracy. They are now our ally, and we cannot give them the impression that they are being coerced into alliance with us," Emusheguta Negutu expressed.

"How many men would this demand? What can we expect from them?" King Buka inquired, looking to his army chief, who, after formalities, proceeded. "Indemba has less than 300 men of war. I will recommend 1,500 men at the initial. Our ally Oman is in mourning, therefore we cannot require much of them. 250 Omanians should suffice. Your Majesty has over 18,000 capable men of war for an army, and filling the deficit to this cause would put your kingdom at no apparent risk. Besides, between Wa-Zanga and Indemba is only 2 days military march."

The king, satisfied with the counsel of his two officials, turned to his treasurer and commanded him to make provisions for the allied armies. He also commanded the army commander to dispatch a 10 man cavalry to Oman with directives for the Omanian troop to immediately meet with his men on the outskirts of Indemba. The treasurer will make provision in gold for the Omanian troop, and the cavalry takes it with them. The men leave at first light, therefore, the treasurer and commander will spend the night working. They are relieved by the king to execute the urgent tasks on their tables. Negutu and the scribe remain with the king to ready a response for Tuoza, and a letter to Governor Yaw Edusei.

The Wa-Zanga cavalry arrives in Oman before Noon of the third day of their journey. They requested audience with the governor and made special request of Tuoza's presence. Governor Yaw Edusei summoned the former administrator. The governor sat in the hall with Tuoza and the leader of the cavalry, who quickly removed two letters from within his European-made woolen jacket. He presented the letters, wrapped and bearing the royal seal of King Buka, to the Yaw and Tuoza. Yaw ordered Tuoza to read both letters, which the latter did, but with so much effort, being unsure of the content of the letter addressed to him. But at the end, he could smile. The letter to him was simply a warm response from Buka to him, informing him that Wa-Zanga will keep to its pledge to ally with Oman. The governor's letter bore Buka's condolences, and decision to muster an ally army against Indemba for the freedom of Nana Serwaa. Yaw Edusei could afford a smile.

Couple days ago, Oman ended fasting for the death of the Queen Mother. She was buried on the third day because her spirit was grievous and her body, in spite preservation spices and fragrances, showed signs of decay. The family and the kingdom officials decided on later dates for various observations for Nana Ama Bosotwe. However, upon request from Tuoza, Oman waited on response from Wa-Zanga to determine its next call of action. Now, of course, the kingdom is aware it must commit 250 men, whose welfare Wa-Zanga's gold will cover. The governor had Tuoza receive the chest of gold from Buka's lieutenant, and made a call to the portal who swiftly opened the door and entered, collecting the chest from Tuoza.

Within an hour, Oman's army chief had begun mustering his 250 men. They will start leaving for the outskirts of Indemba tonight, escorted by Buka's cavalry. Within four days they will arrive and join forces with the Wa-Zangan army.

Without any incident, both the Omanians and Wa-Zanga armies arrived on the outskirts of Indemba – at their point of meeting, as planned. First to arrive was the Wa-Zangan army, which arrived by mid-morning. The Omanian army, escorted by the Wa-Zangan cavalry, arrived at the point before 1:00PM. After meetings of senior military and civilian bras from both sides, which included Tuoza and Emusheguta Negutu, a delegation was set up. Negutu will have Tuoza as his deputy, and 10 men will escort them into Indemba. They peacefully will request the hand of Nana Serwaa and the other captives with her. They will stress that the captives are important to King Buka of Wa-Zanga, and that the king requests Indemba to release them unconditioinally. Failure to do so before the going down of the sun will provoke an attack by Wa-Zanga that will not be halted until there is no brake left upon another in Indemba, and every one of its citizens is dead.

With such propositions the ally negotiators rode in a carriage into the little country. Nine of their guards rode on horses, and one drove the carriage. As they entered, citizens ran helter-skelter, in spite the slow and peaceful movement. Within a few minutes, 25 armed Indemba men stopped their procession and inquired of their mission. Negutu responded, speaking their dialect fluently. He introduced himself and his comrade Touza, informed the commander that they came in peace and require urgent audience with the chief. The commander asked them to hold on, while he went aside and spoke with one of his men. Immediately, the man the commander spoke with headed for the chief's residence. The commander returned and informed his guest that he has sent word to the chief, who will decide if or not to see them. Almost 15 minutes elapsed before the man returned and the commander again went aside with him. With haste the commander left that messenger and came to the window of the carriage where Negutu sat. "You will follow" he said, and motioned to his men who divided themselves into two groups, walking behind and before their guests.

On Indemba's outskirts, the men of war waited impatiently for an assault. Every minute the negotiators spent away appeared to them ten times as much. For them, a battle was impending, and for such their bloods were warming. Exactly 27 minutes passed, before they spotted the negotiators' train riding jubilantly toward them. Then, there was a sight more startling. There is another carriage, and that is already recognized by some of the troop – Wa-Zangans and Omanians, who saw it and who rode by it. It is Nana Serwaa's. The princess Serwaa and her two servants, and the six guards that were taken into captivity, have been released without a shot of gun or bow. As the negotiators arrived with Nana Serwaa and party, and the sight was confirmed to the troop, as eager as they were for battle, they were moved by compassion when they set their eyes on the Omanian princess, who came out of her carriage by request of Tuoza. And they shouted a great shout of victory.

CHAPTER VII

T HROUGH AN INTERPRETER, THE PRINCESS addressed the troop, expressing her gratitude and moving the soldiers and leaders to tears.

"Wa-Zanga!" she shouted with sustained voice. "You have left your homes and families and have come to rescue a stranger. From the highest, even to the lowest, Wa-Zanga has shown me profound kindness and have committed to this daring sacrifice of its noble sons for my sake. The houses of my father and mother combined cannot reward you satisfactorily. All of the gold of Obuasi, if I could, I would freely give to you, and yet, I will still feel a mountain of debt on my shoulders towards you. Wa-Zanga, what can I give you! If I could multiply myself, I would be that great wife to every bachelor here present, and a dozen more wives to King Buka. And, if I were gold, I would gladly fill up your purses and meet your every need until there was none. But what am I? The dagger in the heart of my father who had wanted a boy in my stead, the end of hope for my mother whose hopes I crashed. And, even more, I am the wife of a man the gods deprive of me, carrying a seed in my womb of whom I am afraid the gods have assigned a much darker path than mine. No, I can give you nothing, but the gratitude of my heart. Yes, in spite of all the evils the gods have apportioned me, my heart feels a deep emotion of gratitude to you and the king. So my heart, which the gods, I believe, have not touched, or have never yet, blesses you. O! Wa-Zanga, my heart blesses you! Long live Wa-Zanga! Long live King Buka! Long live Emusheguta Negutu!"

The men of war looked on and listened, pitied the princess, yet took warmth from her blessings, and shouted cheers and applauded the speaker.

Turning to Tuoza, she asked, "Do we leave for Oman today?" "As you wish, Your Majesty. 250 of Oman's finest men of war are here to lead you home. Also, our friends, Wa-Zanga, are sure to give us escort to ensure you arrive home safely. Only speak the words, and that will be the order which these men follow. For, you are the princess, and more so, I perceive that the gods need you take charge of your destiny. Lead us, therefore, Your Majesty," Tuoza concluded with a bow.

With her eyes fixed towards the sky, Nana Serwaa shouted "Oman, Oman, Oman, rise! Oman rises again!" Then she lowered her eyes, and spoke to the Omanians who were making their way to the front. "I will make great demands of you, but nothing you could not have done for my father, and nothing you cannot do for me. We leave for Oman today! There will be neither sleeping nor resting, until I set my eyes on Oman."

Negutu and the commander of the Wa-Zangan troop stepped forward, and the commander ordered a battalion of 200 soldiers to escort the princess. Negutu assured the princess, who had Tuoza at her side that Wa-Zanga stands as an ally of Oman. He summarized the plan of the Great League, and reminded the princess that the security and prosperity of any one kingdom lay in its bond to a strong union of kingdoms. And to that the princess nodded, and further pledged that she was open to supporting any cause in the common interest of both kingdoms. When such and such matters were discussed and the procession ready, the princess was informed. She bade Negutu and the returning Wa-Zangan troop farewell, while she called on the gods to do this favor, if but this one kindness – to lead her and these soldiers home, and safely return the escort to their country.

The princess ordered the procession in motion. Tuoza signaled to the commanding officer, who, with a certain appearance of confusion, gave directives to the ally troops leading the princess home. As the men leading the train started off, the CO, half bent, beckoned to Nana Serwaa to enter the carriage. But the princess said no word. She only just started walking behind the leading troop. Her servants rushed out of the carriage and joined her. Then, with haste the CO issued final instructions to his men, and the entire train was in motion.

Nana Serwaa and her troop began this journey shortly before 4:00PM, and made no stop until after midnight and Touza's persistent plea with the princess for the latter to take a rest. He acknowledged she was in the right to follow her heart and lead on without rest, but for the unborn she carried in her womb, he implored her to have, if even, a respite. The princess' carriage was taken to a designated spot, after the camp was set up. She requested her maidservants to join her in the carriage, but Tuoza interrupted. "Kindly go on alone yet until I speak with them. I know they are kind, but they are not our people, and I need must ask them a few questions to ensure your safety, if you may." The queen consented, and went ahead to the carriage escorted by an Omanian guard. As they approached unto the carriage, within a few feet distance, the guard bade the princess goodnight.

As the princess Serwaa climbed into the carriage, she realized somebody was there before she could take a seat. She panicked and shouted "who is this!?" Instantly, a relaxed male voice replied, "Yaw." "It is well! I am fine!" Nana Serwaa shouted to the apparently alarmed soldiers. But the COs of both ally troops were aware of this set up, and Tuoza and other Omanian soldiers knew of it too. Yaw Edusei had journeyed with the ally troop from Oman. He was in total disguise and only a few of the troop, and Tuoza, were aware of his presence from Oman through. He was in the muster when his wife addressed both troops of the ally army. When he heard her stir up the spirits of the Omanian troop, he wished to reveal himself and lift her off the ground into the air. He'd thought of hugging and kissing her. He had wished of vanishing home with her. Yes, many things he wished, including that her mother were alive. But he bitterly reminded himself that his wishes were unrealistic, and that there was time and space here only for practicable ideas. So he thanked himself for making this trip, and directed his focus on leading his wife and troop home through the CO.

The night was dark and cold and breezy. The moon and stars hid themselves from the dreadful news the Omanian governor will deliver tonight. After an intimate long hug and kisses, the governor painted for his lover The Spectacle. Yaw assured Nana Serwaa that shortly, with Wa-Zanaga-Oman alliance, he will have a leverage in getting Ashanti into the Great League, even against possible opposition from Mampong which is very influential in Ashanti affairs. Of course, he can expect no support from Mampong with his decision to put away his first wife Nana Yaa, a daughter of the ruling house of Mampong. But being happily alone with Nana Serwaa and their children was better than anything Mampong could offer. A child is on the way, a boy child hopefully. They will have many sons and daughters, and Oman will have a chief place in the region. Once more, through his mediation, Ashanti will grant Oman full sovereignty and cancel the annual levy. Yaw articulated all that and more to his wife, painting for her a most beautiful and optimistic picture of life – The Spectacle.

Then the governor held her tighter in his arms, and for a while spoke no word. He let the silence have its moment, while he gathered courage to inform Nana Serwaa Berimah of the death of her mother. "A lot has happened to you and Oman and, I must add, to me. But we have to move on and embrace the great path the gods have carved out before us. There is much to grief for, but, fair to the gods, there is much to be grateful for. The gods have given us a child, even the one you carry; but, by their will, they wrought you a great cut to the heart. Your mother..." The princess interrupted Yaw, almost shouting "is my mother dead!?"

"Yes, woman of my heart," he answered. She screamed sharply, the teenage still present in the voice. And screamed a few more times, then began calling out memories with her mother. Her husband knew right not to stop her from crying. He allowed her on, and she cried and grieved and lamented an hour over. All Yaw did was hug her tighter and kissed her over and over. Then, as her weeping subsided, he give her details of her mother's death and burial, and the processions that are to follow. More tears and breakdown, until she fell asleep in the arms she has longed for these many days and nights.

As she slept, Nana Serwaa dreamed a strange dream. She saw the faces of many Omanians as they gathered singing and drumming. She could not get the words of the song, but they appeared to her to be one of mocking. As the song became louder and the drumming bursting to the point of her losing her hearing, she saw the singers, drummers and a great many people march outside of Oman. Of the people were happy ones that danced to the music, and others that wept and walked dejectedly. Then, as the procession arrived at the main road in and out of Oman, she saw herself standing alone, wretchedly dressed, with her back turned to the marchers. She behind over her shoulders hoping to see Yaw, but he was not. Then, finally, she heard a loud chant of many voice "Go! Go! Nana Srerwaa, Go!" At that thundering call, she jumped from bed and realized the one man she did not see in her dream was there with her; she was asleep in his lap and arms.

The last night in Indemba, she dreamed the same dream. And the next day she gained her freedom. Tonight, she dreams the dream again. What can that mean? Upon hearing the dream, Yaw encourages her that it may be foul spirits trying to bind her soul with sorrow. If the dream was any ill, she would not be on her way home. Besides, who would banish her from Oman, the very land of her fathers? Who would banish her from Oman, the land she had been soul ruler of, were it not for Ashanti? Thus did he reasoned with her, and she was encouraged.

Four days of travel, and the Omanian train safely arrives home. Nana Serwaa needs rest, but now is not the time. The princess will be the spectacle of a parade that is to cover the entire city grounds of the kingdom. She will be paraded with every musical instrument including drums, but the march will not carry its customary loud plays. Oman is bereaved. But quietly as possible, the princess will receive a welcome from her countrymen as she is taken to the four corners of the city. And on the morrow, the priests will perform the thanksgiving rituals for her safe return.

The parade had a turnout bigger than any in the history of Oman. From old to ageing, from youth to children, male and female, there hardly was a soul capable of walking that did not come out of their house unto the streets at the least, to greet the princess. And the vast majority of the city's residents and villagers came and joined in the parade. From some time past 3:00PM, the parade concluded at 6:30, just at twilight. However, thousands spent the night in the palace grounds, uniting with the royal family and officials in celebrating the demise of the Queen Mother. For tonight, the custom prevails. The time of mourning is over, since the deceased is buried. The princess cannot cry, she can only mourn her mother quietly. Tears after burial is bad luck. Now Oman will celebrate the life the dead woman lived. There will be music and food and wine. Perhaps, the cultural display will aid the bereaved family, Nana Serwaa especially, cope with their loss. So the entire royal family, the governor and royal officials, sat up on the long L-shaped porch, as Oman celebrated the life of Nana Ama Bosomtwe - the Queen Mother. Eating and drinking and music and cultural display, which lasted until day break, crowned the celebration. But Princess Serwaa retired to bed before midnight.

Her first three nights back home, Nana Serwaa Berimah dreamed the frightening dream of people singing and chanting against her to leave Oman. Each night the dream was exactly the same, but each morning the feeling grew more real and in fact stranger to the princess. She will accept the governor's encouragement no further. She asks to see the priest, who will inquire of the gods the meaning of her dreams, or rather, the visions the very gods have visited her with night after night.

After breakfast today, the chief priest is summoned at the palace. Privately, the couple sat with him in the governor's office. After the governor welcomed the chief spiritual leader of Oman and thanked him for honoring his invitation to the palace at so short a notice, he turned to his wife and asked her to inform the priest of the matters of her dream.

"For a fifth straight night, Okomfo (priest), I have had a strange dream. Each time I awake, my soul is overwhelmed with sadness, and I get the feeling that it is more than a mere dream," she paused, trying to gather herself. At that point the priest interrupted "the gods give you strength. What is the dream?"

"I see the faces many Omanians known to me. They sing, they drum, and they dance, as they make their way out of the city. The words of the songs I never understand, though I'm certain they speak our tongue. And in my spirit I perceive that they mock me. But the procession is an odd mix of mockers and sympathizers. I do not know if I am with the marchers or not, but I see them proceed to the entrance, or rather, the way out of the city. At the exit, I see myself wretched and alone with my back turned towards Oman and the great crowd. Always, I'm unable to turn, except a twist of my head over my shoulders, hoping for a rescuer in Nana Yaw. For it seems like I am being fought against. But I never see him. I see only the same faces, and worse, I hear the crowd roar like thunder "Go! Go! Nana Serwaa go!" Tell me, Okomfor, what does that mean?"

The priest looked up and recited an incantation. Then with an unusual speed he let his head down into his palms. After a handful of seconds, he stood up, and without a word, walked out of the room. The princess is afraid. Before now, she was afraid, but she was more confused than afraid. However, with the priest's action, her confusion instantly fades away. It is only obvious that the meaning to her dream is terrible as the feelings that lingers with her at waking. Perhaps, there is not a mere meaning, but the dream itself is an event of the future. But why will Oman do such a thing to Nana Serwaa Berimah? And even so, when will this be?

The spiritual head of Oman left the royal pair without saying a word. The governor wishes to speak, to at least encourage the princess, but as he sits deep in his seat, he cannot fathom the words that may relieve his wife of her fears. For himself is already taken by fear and confusion. And his wife, free of her confusion, only asks why and when? As her husband sinks in his fear and confusion, the poor girl runs out the doors to heads to her chamber. Her mother and father are no more. Her husband is unable to help her, and the priest of the land has walked out on her. But no sooner had the latter thought entered her mind than she dismissed it, realizing rather that Okomfor is a priest of the gods. He was predisposed to do the gods bidding, and it mattered little to him if the gods wrought some great evil on humanity. The priest is merely an instrument of the gods. He translates them to the people, and interpret the people to them. But the latter is largely a formality. Or, do the gods change their minds or words because humans are unable to endure the effect? Are not our enjoyment and suffering the crafting of the gods? What is human, then, that we should determine our destiny or the course thereof, or even seek to avoid a path laid out for us. We can only live out what the gods have apportioned for us, and that we are wont to know except they or their messengers allow us. And why should they that we know of the evil that is intended for us, if there is no chance of avoiding the fate. Or do the gods simply enjoy tormenting us with the dread that destiny holds in store for us? Is not the direct experience suffering enough?

So soon had the months gone by, and the princess and governor forgot all about the dreams. They appear to Nana Serwaa no more, never since the high priest's visit. He spiritualist said nothing, but could he have done something? Perhaps he interceded with the gods, and they have spared the princess the possible tragic outcome of her dreams. Or at least, they have delivered her from the torturing night vision.

Today the princess' time for delivery is due, and Oman expects a son. So does the governor. Three women – the nurse and maid from Wa-Zanga and the esteemed Nana Adjoa, the veteran midwife of Oman who delivered Nana Serwaa into the world nearly 18 years ago, attend to the princess. Today, though, the amiably experienced practitioner hopes that the gods bless her hands to deliver into the word and Oman a male child to continue the Berimah dynasty.

An hour passed by and the patient is unable to push the child. Nana Adjoa then observes that the baby is in a transverse breech. She made the sign to the two women, but only maid could not understand. The Wa-Zangan nurse panicked. There was not nothing to be done, except wait and see if goes gets into normal position. At least that is what the stranger nurse understood. But here in Oman, they did not leave this situation to chance. For to leave such a matter in the hands of chance was to risk the life of not just the baby but the mother. The experienced Omanian nurse asked the maid to bring her bag closer. She then instructed the maid to get out the sculpted infant and lay it head down on the princess' abdomen. The sculpture was carved from the sacred Ehunumobro Dua (Tree of Mercy). In Akan midwifery, if a pregnant woman has difficulty with delivery, the midwife applied the tree of mercy, through ingestion of its solution, laying it on the patient or as the particular case dictated. They believe that the god of mercy comes to aid the suffering woman by allowing her to bring forth the child. And for centuries Akan midwives have known and concealed this from the world.

Within few minutes of the sculpture on her tummy, Nana Serwaa screamed, and the midwife and co knew that the time was now. The baby had followed the pattern of the image on its mother's belly, swiftly abandoning its breech and assuming a normal position for safe delivery. And as the baby made its way out, or rather, the mother delivered it, the assist team watched anxiously. They waited for the sex to be revealed. Now, with Nana Serwaa apparently safe and fine, the sex of the infant is all that matters. Then, here the baby's sex is out, but just as it is revealed, there is a twist. There will no rejoicing for the male child. The infant appears instantly dead. Fully delivered now, but there is no pulse. And the room is dead silent; the women communicate with bodily expression to each other. The princess seems to have fallen asleep from exhaustion, but they are wary of bringing this awful incident to her knowledge. At least not until she is fully recuperated.

At the door of the princess' chambers two of her sisters and members of the royal family stand by for the news. They are here to get the news of a boy child and broadcast it to Oman which will burst into singing and dancing and praise to the gods for finally granting a male child to the Berimahs. And in his chambers Yaw Edusei lays on his bed, having imagined a dozen times these words of the midwife: "Obirempong, I am happy to inform you that your wife has successfully given birth to a male child." But those are hopeless imaginings, as the news hits him, and the royal family and Oman that the princess delivered a male child, but the infant died at birth.

The sorrow and pain and grief felt in the kingdom today has never been and never will be. At the rising of the expectations of these people, the gods have ordained it otherwise. Oman has only gone from misery to greater misery. The young girl took comfort and pride in making Yaw Edusei a father, finally, but the gods have willed otherwise. When a daughter finally believed the gods have made her the bearer of a male child in the male-barren Berimah family, her expectancy is cut short. Nana Serwaa will not rejoice, but sorrow. Yaw Edusei cannot boast, he is humbled. And Oman is wont to celebrate, but mourn.

Childlessness was not to be condoned in marriage; especially not among the Akan people of the regions, of which were those of Ashanti and Oman. Nana Yaa, the first wife of Nana Yaw Edusei is aware that their marriage only survived the many years it did because of the office and estate of her family. But to be married is one thing, and to enjoy the love of a husband is absolutely another. The past few years, particularly her stay in Oman, reflected that every bit. For her husband was in love with another woman – Nana Serwaa Berimaah, and with a child expected between the pair, Nana Yaa became an angry woman. She was filled with rage and jealousy, and Yaw Edusei was certain she would stop at nothing to redeem her place. Therefore he sent her away, hoping to secure his new wife and expected child and the children to follow.

But with the death of his child at birth, the governor wonders if he rather is the problem, the one cursed of the gods, and not his first wife. Nana Yaa never conceived. Nana Serwaa conceived and give birth to a child, who only saw the light of day and returned to the land of darkness. Barrenness is uncommon, if it exists at all, in Mampong, the home of Nana Yaa. The house of Berimah is not familiar with it either. And neither is this barrenness of commonplace in his family. It might be the gods are angry with him because of a transgression he has committed that is unknown to him. Perhaps, because of that, the gods shut the womb of Nana Yaa and has frustrated the labor of Nana Serwaa.

It has been three months since Nana Serwaa lost her baby. And her husband is yet to visit her chambers or invite her to his. The governor loves his wife still, but he is afraid his life is trapped or marked out by the gods for misfortune, and he is only mindful to protect the woman he loves. Yet ignoring or avoiding her just hurts. She feels rejected by Nana Yaw, and a great sense of dejection has overshadowed her. The past two days she requested a meeting with him, but he has turned her down. He twice promised to visit her but never honored his words. She will request a meeting no more. Instead, she will demand one, and rather than expect him over, she will call on him at his chambers tonight.

A short while after dinner in her chambers, Nana Serwaa Berimah did the unusual. As a kid she never crept about; she boldly went where she pleased in this palace built by her grandfather, the very house wherein she was born and raised, and has lived and married. Tonight she cannot help but giggle at the thought of sneaking her way to the governor's chamber. Then thoughts of her parents came rushing into her mind, but she dismissed them. Now is not the time to deal with worries or memories. To be counted a living evokes in every person a feeling of commitment to a purpose greater than one's self. Her sense of purpose, the princess believes, is to reignite the torch of the Berimah Dynasty. And that can only be accomplished by her bringing into this world a male child. Yes, everything relies on her birthing a male child, but in the hands of the gods are such things. Humans are free to dream, and the gods are unrestricted by our aspirations as they distribute to all peoples whatever they would.

The guard at the governor's entrance recognized the Omanian princess in the half illuminated hallway as she approached. He jumped to his feet and asked her, almost whispering for fear of disturbing the governor, "is everything alright, Your Majesty?" "I will see the governor" she said softly but forcefully. The guard, without a word, hit on the door with codes designed by Yaw

Edusei himself. Hearing the knock, the governor knows his wife is here. He sounded a code from within, and the guard said goodnight to the princess and excused himself to the living room. The governor opened the door and let his wife in, then shut and locked the door.

Nana Serwaa had scarcely sat down before her first question was out: "are you disappointed in me?" "Na..." "Where is the love you introduced me to?" she cut him off. "A child is all you hoped for from me and now that I failed to grant your desire, you have shut the doors of your life against me. I have become like Nana Yaa in your eyes, and who knows, maybe worse! I am sorr..." "You have no reason to be sorry!" Yaw interrupted. "You speak out of the bitterness of your soul. You have entertained ill thoughts, and that is my fault! But, do you pause to listen to the music of your heart; the harmony of the instruments and the sweetness of the voice that sings? Are not the words of the song all about the beauty of our love, the tightness of our bond, the courage of our dream and the daring of our actions? The heart of our relationship is a lion's and our wings a mighty eagle's. We can surmount the highest obstacles. If the gods of our fathers are inclined to abandon us, or worse, bestow bad luck upon us, we will not despair! Contrarily, we will rise up and burn bright with the light of our hopes and dreams, and to our generation and many more to come, we will be the light that shows the way."

He sat by her at the bed foot, took her right hand in his left, and stared into the wall. Then he released her hand and fixed his palm and fingers on her abdomen, and pull her that she dropped into the bed with him. They lay on their backs with their feet on the carpet, while Yaw spoke again, reassuring her of his love. He explained his reasons for avoiding her, but promised her that if she would, they will achieve the world. And Nana Serwaa, as strong-will as himself, graciously obliged. And their hopes and dreams were instantly rekindled. They promised each other sons, and spoke for hours about their children ruling Oman and the great Ashanti Empire. Then, as they traveled through their dream plans, the warmth of their bodies against each other sparked a great flame of passion that consumed the couple in blissful intimacy. They burned away. But, with the morning comes the mystery: out of their ashes, like the phoenix, they are revived.

CHAPTER VIII

O MAN PLAYS HOST TO A meeting of the Great League. For three days leaders from 6 kingdoms and chiefdoms have been meeting here in the Omanian capital. This evening, the princess and governor hosts the guests at a formal dinner in the great guest hall built by the late king a year before his demise. Nana Berimah built it for the purpose of meeting and banquet. Tonight, for the first time, the banquet section will be used. Prominent among the guests are Otumfuo Nana Prempeh II, Ashantihene and King Buka of Wa-Zanga.

But shortly after the dinner got underway, the expected attractions – the Ashantihene Nana Prempeh II and King Buka, were overshadowed by Nana Serwaa's sudden illness. The princess collapsed and fell to the ground while reaching for her seat. As soon as she was resuscitated, the governor ordered that she be taken home and checked and monitored by her nurse.

The princess diagnosis, to her very surprise, was pregnancy. She was, again, with child. Nana Serwaa could not wait for Yaw to get home. A messenger was dispatched with the message. She was certain it will at least lift his spirit after causing him and their guests an apparent panic. Also, the princess expects that, with the news, their guests will relax and feast without worrying about the hostess.

As the months went by, the princess became more anxious. And so did the governor and all of Oman. She desires to hold a child – a male child in her arms and present him to her husband. He longs for a child he can call his own, an answer to his scorners. And they crave a boy, a security of the Berimah's royalty.

Oman's chief midwife and the princess servants attended to her while she gave birth for the second time. They hope that the time is now, when the gods return to Oman. For long during the days of King Berimah, when his wife gave him one girl after another, many citizens believed the gods had departed the kingdom. Some even believed that King Berimah siined against the gods, but none could mention it to even his brother for fear of the king who was widely revered by Oman. Perhaps the gods are near, seeing the princess first child was a boy, though he died at birth. Or rather, the gods are seeking to inflict the house of Berimah with greater sorrow by making them seem closer. Whatever, these women know it is a matter of minutes, at worse hours, and they will know the fate of the princess and the kingdom.

Within 18 minutes, Nana Serwaa Berimah was delivered of her child. This time, it was a boy child, but still born. The delivery team could not conceal their disappointment with their looks. At that, the princess, using her elbows to support the suspense of her upper body, demanded an answer. And with the response, she fell back into her bed, fainted.

The chief priest visited the governor three days after another unsuccessful delivery by the princess. "The princess is cursed! She is destined to bring pain and suffering upon this land. It is the will of the gods that she be banished, and Oman be spared the destruction embedded in her destiny. Until this woman is expelled from this kingdom, the wrath of the gods will be upon the people, including the royal house. Three months from today, I will perform her banishment ceremony. Until then, you will have communion with her. She must live separately and keep indoors.

All of her meals must be served her within her room. Her bath bucket must not be used by anyone. The words of the gods!" Nana Yaw heard those words from the priest, and replied not a word. The priest walked out of the governor's office, and went to the back of the palace to meet the chief servant of the house. He narrated the same message he gave the governor. Then, finally, he raced across from the palace to the administrative building, where he greeted and waved with the same words. Then to his shrine he returned.

The three months went by rather slow for Nana Serwaa. She was tormented by the delay of a punishment that was imminent. If she could not avoid it, she embraced it. This, indeed, is the dream that tormented her those night. And the priest, understanding the dread of her fate, had refused to comment. The gods had already spoken.

She cried day and night. She cried for her children, for her husband, and for her family. She will see them no more, and not because she wills to, but because the gods have purposed so. She leaves the land of her fathers and journeys to where she knows not. But she must go, that the people she loves might be spared her curse.

The chief priest is out again, but today with his team. They will escort the princess of Oman and wife of its governor Nana Yaw Edusei, out of the kingdom. Or rather bluntly, today, the men from the shrine will lead Oman in the banishment of its princess. They invite her out, and right in the palace square the priests and their attendants performed the ceremony. Aside the governor who asked to be excused, the rank and file of Oman was present. And when the ceremony was concluded, the priest walked ahead, Nana Serwaa followed, then went the people of Oman.

The events of her dreams flashed! With the exception of the priests, everything here was known to her. From faces and expressions to garments worn by the people, Nana Serwaa saw it all in her dreams. The priests presented her the very wretched dress she wore in the dream, and that she wore before the ceremony. Now the songs and drumming...the mocking... She looks back over her left shoulder to see if, perhaps, Yaw has come to her aid. But he had not. He could not. And here, finally, after the long march out of the city comes the chanting "Go! Go! Nana Serwaa go!" At that moment, at the exit of the city, her heart broke, and so did the fountain of her tears. Ironically, Oman commanded, and the princess submitted.

Nana Serwaa Berimah, the princess and heir apparent to the Berimah throne, is banished from Oman, the land of her ancestors. She had walked from mid-morning to the going down of the sun. Her mind has wandered back to her kingdom, while her body, almost absently, walked these lonely stretches, passing towns and villages. And she sang as well, even unconsciously, songs learned from her mother. She knows her parents are somewhere watching over her. Or perhaps, they simply are just watching her. For the latter tells of them being able to see her, but yet unable to help. And that certainly must be the case here. How else could their daughter and only hope be banished from the very kingdom they built with their sweat and blood, walking many barren and desolate stretches at the peril of her own life?

The human spirit may be capable of the impossible, but there is limit to the denials of our bodies. She had walked a score of miles in an average temperature of 99 degrees. She had drank no water and eaten no food. The custom of banishment did not make such provisions. She need must make a stop at the nearest village or town. She has need of rest, of water and food, and of accommodation.

She braced herself for the next village or town. She could not tell how near or far it is, but she is prepared to continue her walk in the opposite direction of Oman. Earlier, she passed several people, but she only now recollects that. At the time her mind was deep in thoughts. But as the sun sets and her journey is unending, she becomes more conscious of the road and her surroundings. She has come across nobody for nearly an hour, and that unsettles the princess. She frightened. Her heart skips and beat and then begins racing uncontrollably. Somebody must be watching. But the poor girl cares little about someone watching her as she is concerned with their motive. She instinctively started to run, looking back and sideways. Then she heard a voice – a shout, and found that there are, in fact, people. A man calling and running behind her, then, another two. She ran as fast as she could, and shouted as loudly as her famished body could permit. But the men were too quick for her, and within a minute one of her chasers approached unto her and pulled her by the back of her shabby dress. She fell to the ground with him.

The three men lifted the princess and ran with her into the bushes, covering her mouth for fear of possible alarm. And there, concealed by the bushes, the three men molested the princess of Oman – the wife of Nana Yaw Edusei. She has gone to Wa-Zanga and maintained her dignity. All through her growing up she practiced chastity, and as a wife she demonstrated morality. As much as has depended on her, she had been a proud daughter of her parents in their life and death. And today, if they are watching her, they know that she stands true to the virtues they imparted to her; however, circumstances totally beyond her control have subjected her to victimization of three uncultured and graceless abusers. Then, they ran off, leaving the lifeless girl in the bush.

During the banishment ceremony in the palace square, Yaw Edusei watched through the windows. He cried out in frustration to the gods of his ancestors. He was not sure they will answer him at this crucial moment, but he could not withhold himself from succumbing to the pains of the pin that has pierced him deeper and deeper each day since the banishment of his wife was announced. On the day of the banishment announcement, he had sent to Kumasi to the Queen Mother Asantehemaa Yaa Akyaa, mother of the exiled king Otumfuo Prempeh I. The governor requested that the Queen Mother appoint a new governor to run Ashanti affairs in Oman. He intends to return to Kumasi and live out his days quietly.

His request was honored, and he was not the least disappointed that Ashanti showed no inclination to interfere with the Omanian tradition. At least, he was allowed to stay until the banishment as he had additionally requested.

When the banishment ceremony concluded, the officials and chief members of the Omanian royal family assembled in the hall of the palace. Governor Nana Yaw Edusei introduced the guests from Kumasi. They arrived during the night. Then, he explained that Ashanti has granted his resignation. He lauded the officials and members of the royal family for their support over the years, and indicated his respect for their customs. However, there was no meaning to life anymore for him, especially not in Oman. He then introduced his cousin and successor: "Today Ashanti officially relieves me of my office and have appointed in my stead Nana Kwadwo Antwi." Then he pleaded with them to accord him due respect and support. When he was done speaking and the Omanian officials and members of the royal family, Yaw Edusei and his direct staff departed for Kumasi.

On her way to their way to the farm, Adwoa Pomaa and her teenage son picked wild fruits that dropped from the trees. A little way from their farm, as they approached one of such trees, the young boy noticed the feet of a human and pointed his mother in the direction. They moved slowly toward the feet and realized it was a whole figure of a young woman covered in blood. She appeared lifeless, but the experienced woman felt otherwise. The old woman prevented her son from getting closer with the hand. She stepped forward, took off her over garment, laid it on the young woman, from her shoulders past her knees. Then Adwoa Pomaa examined the body and found that the she was still alive. She instructed her son to pour water from their jug into her hands, and she sprinkled it on the face of the still woman. But to no avail. Then she requested her son to wait while she went and fetched herb she was certain would revive the sick.

She returned a short while later, washed the leaves she brought, rubbed them in the palm of her hands until their fluid began to seep out. She took the formed ball from her palms and squeezed it into both nostrils of the sick, who sneezed a few seconds later. Then a few more sneezes, and the young woman opened her eyes. She seemed confused and frightened, but Adwoa Pomaa peaceful smile and wave of the hand assured her that she was safe.

The old woman and her son gave the stranger water, and later food. They were amazed the woman spoke Twi. And though she did not say yet what country she came from, she informed them of the circumstances of her rape. And they took pity on her and invited her home with them. "You can lodge with us for as long as you may," said the older woman to the younger one.

March 27, 1905 will go down in Nana Serwaa's memories as the darkest day. It was the day of both her banishment and rape. However, her host has encouraged her that that is her past, and that there are many more years filled with happiness ahead of the young woman. But she found that Nana Serwaa was reluctant to be comforted. Therefore she inquired of the stranger why she was out here in a strange country. And the princess narrated her ordeals to her host, who herself broke down and found herself in the darkness and gloominess of the speaker. Yet she managed her way out and cheered the young woman "You bear the strength of the gods themselves. For who else could have borne such miseries and be alive. The gods might have caused you excruciating suffering, but I trust they will reward you in proportion to your woes."

Nana Serwaa quickly settled in at Akorda Suyanni. Against the imploring of her host she has persistently joined the pair to the farm. After all, Adwoa Pomaa was a widow and lived alone with her son. If she lived with them, she had to be of help. This was a humble home and family, not a palace and the Berimahs. Gone are the days when she was a princess. She has accepted the actuality of her circumstances. Here in this country, she is known truly to her host; but for the rest of Akorda Suyanni, she is an orphan who ran away from mistreatment of her relatives.

Nana Yaw Edusei Arrived in Kumasi after six days of traveling. He went home to his mother. He divorced his wife and she had returned to her family. She can marry no more, and he has neither the willingness nor the courage to enter into another. Also, Yaw is determined to have no involvement whatsoever in the fragile underground politics of Ashanti. The British control of affairs here in the capital compels the Ashantis to act secretly, and through the numerous meetings, trouble is brewing. Brewing for any potential leader in the now British protectorate. So the warrior and former governor of Oman will live his day to day as an ordinary man, in the very house he grew up from. Sadly, and he is aware, there is no growing up from here anymore. And though he is somewhat young, the state of affairs in Kumasi and Ashanti will only confine him home for as many years as it continues.

About a month in Akorda Suyanni, the Berimah girl is found with child. She is a month pregnant. And this does not evoke joy but confusion. If a woman is with child, there must be a father, dead or alive. But Nana Serwaa cannot determine the father of her child. Her host consoles her that the man responsible for her pregnancy is known to the gods. Yet, for the poor girl, what does that matter? The gods may know, but she lives among humans and not the gods. The past weeks she had found happiness, however differently, in this strange country. But good times don't last for Nana Serwaa. At least not since she was a maiden.

As the months went by and Nana Serwaa's delivery time drew near, Adwoa Pomaa spent each day at home with Nana Serwaa. She sent her son out to the farm with other young boys and girls. The old woman worked day and night to lift the spirit of the young woman who fears the fate of her past two pregnancies hunts her still. In spite the latter's excessive pessimism about her pregnancy and life in general, the earlier keeps her optimistic view on life and remains hopeful that this time the girl will put to bed safely. But it was much more than successful delivery. For Nana Serwaa, safety of birth and the issue of her child's father were equally important; she could found it impossible detach the one from the other. Yet, her hosts persists, day after day and night after night, that she takes on her challenges one at a time; now is the time to focus on the child. When the child is born, she may concern herself with the matters of its father. "What does it matter, Serwaa, if the gods bless you with a child to comfort you in your afflictions? Must there be a father before you accept and love and live with the very child that is as much a part of you as it may be of anyone? If the gods show you kindness in this pregnancy, do, my daughter, show yourself and the child equal compassion," Adwoa Pomaa beseeched of her guest.

Five years went by since Nana Serwaa gave birth to her son. She named him Nana Yaw Edusei Berimah. She was raped by three men, certainly. But how could the child bear the very birth mark of Nana Yaw Edusei, and on the very same spot of the body. It was so compelling that she recounted to her host the events of her last night in Oman. Against the warnings of the high priest, her husband visited her that night and took her to his chambers.

He was resigning his office and returning to Kumasi, while she was being banished, on the following day. They will never see again, and so she was happy he visited her room. They put aside their fears and questions and allowed themselves to indulge in the sea of their great love – in the fire of their passion. For one last time, they willed, and burned! But unlike other times, the phoenixes rose out of their ashes and reincarnated long before day broke. They could not allow themselves to be noticed.

The two women are in Kumasi, seeking Yaw Edusei. They will have no difficulty finding him, in spite a commonplace skepticism because of the political situation in the kingdom. They had asked only at a second home, and they were given a young man to escort them to where her husband resides. As they approach the house, a man ran to meet them. He was a few feet away from them before Nana Serwaa lifted her head and realized that her husband was just before her. He approached unto them, lifted the kid into the air, examined him and then let their foreheads touch for several seconds. Then he put the kid down and hugged Nana Serwaa, lifting her off her feet.

There never was a man happier than Yaw Edusei in all Ashanti. And there never will be. By circumstances he put away a wife, lost two children at birth, resigned his position, and lost a second wife to tradition. Life was done, and all his lovers gone. He returned home to live out his days as an ordinary man, seeking to rise no more, for fear the gods might inflict worse harm upon him. Then, having lost all hopes in those great dreams that defined his excellence in training, learning and service, the gods themselves visit him. They give him a son and restore to him his darling wife. Oh, the ways of the gods! They are ever mystery to humans; who can comprehend them.

Nana Yaw Edusei Berimah was barely 18 when Otumfuo Nana Prempeh I, Ashantehene, returned from exile in the Seychelles.

After a few weeks at home, Nana Prempeh I had a hearing on Oman and reinstated his trusted friend and cousin, Nana Yaw the elder, as governor of Oman. Also, he demanded that Oman rescind its decision of the princess' banishment. The grounds for her banishment is now voided by the fact of her son. The king made the decision after consultations with his priests. A priest will accompany Yaw Edusei and his family to Oman.

Three days later, Governor Nana Yaw Edusei, his wife and son head for Oman. Yaw Berimah will return to Kumasi shortly to complete his training and schooling. But now he joins his parents, being the legal grounds for his mother's return home. Messengers, along with a priest of Ashanti, went ahead yesterday. They will meet with Omanian officials, the high priest of Oman and the outgoing governor. The meeting will pave the way for a rousing welcome of the couple back to the kingdom.

Several years ago, when Nana Serwaa Berimah returned home from her captivity, Oman rejoiced. But today, they celebrate. Today is declared holiday in the entire kingdom. Titled and ordinary men and women are crowding the palace square. They have come with their songs and dances, and they are present with gifts for the princess and the boy and the governor. They regret the banishment, but the leaders have explained that it was the doing of the gods, not men. Therefore, Oman is fully present here in the palace square and the main city streets, safe for the incapacitated.

A day's holiday was declared, but three days went by with celebration of the royal couple and the prince. There was food and wine in abundance the three days. There was hardly rest for the ruling family, for the people took turns and played night and day. Also, they praised the gods for showing mercy to Oman and blessing the princess – the house of Berimah, with a male child.

Within a week's time, the returning officials and messengers set off for Kumasi. They took with them the young Berimah who has a year more at the Ashanti Royal Military Academy. His father has negotiated with the throne in Kumasi to grant his son the title of King in Oman. Yaw forfeited so much in the negotiation, including his heirship to the Ashanti throne. But that is only the beginning of how far he is primed to go for his son.

CHAPTER IX

O N OCTOBER 3 1935, ITALY under its fascist leader Benito Mussolini attacked Ethiopia. At 9:03 AM Saturday, October 5, hierarchical nationalists of the British-handicapped Gold Coast legislature in western Africa convened a secret meeting. The 7 legislators present staunchly opposed the breaching of international law by Italy. For a fact, both Italy and Abyssinia were members of the League of Nations. The men in this meeting had expected an open condemnation of Mussolini's Italy by various member countries of the League. It is nearing two full days since the Italian attack, and the League is yet to convene a meeting to halt Italy or go to the aid of Abyssinia, a chattered member of the international body. Abyssinia under its emperor Haile Selassie is considered Africa's beacon of hope for independence.

It was also an open reality that colonialist nations applauded Italy's violation of international laws, suggestive that colonies had to be subject to their colonial masters. And this was at the height of colonial – Great Britain, France, Belgium, Portugal, Germany and Italy scramble to maintain their African colonies. The human and material resources of Africa were of inestimable importance to the very existence of the colonialists in a Europe and Asia steadily falling to German occupation. And most notably, Great Britain and France, the two most popular colonial powers in Africa greatly required alliances with Italy in order to avert Adolf Hitler's invasion of their countries.

The men at the meeting are careful, not just of external knowledge of their meeting, but more mindful of each other. They had converged at this secret location in various disguises, wary of British spies. But who could ascertain if one or more of them was spy for the colonial power. For in a country divided by British influence, and a house created by its discretion, every legislator was a probable spy, or would possibly become an informant in order to protect and or advance his office. The men are in a complete fix how each person will liberally express his opinions on the Italo-Abyssinian war and other issues facing the African continent at large and the Gold Coast in particular.

For over thirty minutes the discussion between these men revolved around the trust factor. And because nobody or any reasoning could safely satisfy such curiosity or rather ease suchlike anxiety, the honorable men unanimously decide on inviting a priest to administer an oath.

Nana Kwaku Owusu, whose ancestor was priest and contemporary of the great Priest and co-founder of the Ashanti Empire, was the selection for the administration of the oath. The priest was in nearby Awukugua, working with other priests in preparation for the Ohum festival which is days away – by the fullness of the moon. A messenger was dispatched and succeeded in returning with the highly revered traditional priest.

The priest – Nana Owusu made himself the conspicuous choice in March in the Ashanti Empire's capital of Kumasi during the Odwera Festival this year. At the festival, he openly spoke against British presence, dominance, and discussed a highly probable future of the Gold Coast free of foreign interference. The secret assembly know they can count on a priest that is not merely concerned about an independent Ashanti state or empire, but that of the entire Gold Coast.

When the priest arrived, he was introduced to the members of the secret assembly by the one man he knew, and that so well. In fact, he was the eight member of this assembly and the initiator. He was not a legislator, but it must be known that he was by reason the most powerful non British in the country. His name was Sir Theophilus Kwakwei Quartey. He was the liaison between the British government and the local Gold Coast ruling council and legislature. His office technically stretched farther, and so did his power. He played chief mediator and liaison between Ashanti and the territories north and the British. In essence, his power and duties far transcended his official title. The introduction was done cordially but swiftly. The men had to get down to business.

No sooner had Nana Kwaku Owusu heard from these politicians than request a bucket of water. The water was brought into the room, the first of three rooms in this mud house at the foot of the hill in this eastern Gold Coast village of Belgoro. No member of the house was present within. Holding in midair his staff engraved with the Adinkra – the symbol representing the Supreme God's (Nyame) omnipotence and omnipresence, he entreated the favor and guidance of the respective abosoms (spirits). As if unconsciously, his staff descended, pointed at the bucket of water that sat less than two feet from him. For a few minutes he spoke and recited incantations intermittently, followed by a lengthy pause. Then, with what appeared a sudden awakening from slumber, or a return of his spirit to his mortal body, he gazed at the faces of the eight men, one after the other, without a word spoken.

Finally the priest, with knees erect, bent over the bucket of water and placed his staff therein with his left hand. And with his right he pulled out a goblet of water. The eight men were startled. There was only a bucket with water in it. Now, there was a goblet. But Nana Owusu continued to face the water as be bent, looking intently into it. Then he handed the cup in the direction parallel to his bent body but to no one in particular. And nobody dared take the cup, not until he mentioned the name of a particular legislator who sat on a stool at his right back. The legislator moved to the front gingerly. This was the audacious Ekow Kutu-Adu. But this was not parliamentary proceedings with men; it was a spiritual business, the very kind the adept legislator was oblivious to. Hon. Kutu-Adu stood a way off from the hand holding the goblet, only close enough for his stretched out hands to take the goblet. Upon repetition of the words of oath after the priest, the legislator was required to drink the water.

So did all of the legislators and Sir Quartey proceeded and swore the oath. And the priest moved on to a more captivating display of patriotism and spiritual power. He informed the eight that he will become the ninth member, not merely because of the magnitude of the matter he has come to know of, but more because he shared their passion for an independent Gold Coast nation and Africa at large. His knowledge of political matters locally and internationally did not surprise these men. Nana Kwaku Owusu is widely famed as the traditional priest *that humbled himself... sat at the feet of the white man to be schooled...* And, as the men sought to come to terms with the priest's daring volunteering, the latter, who now sat on a mat of his own, raised his head looking to the heavens – or rather now the thatch roof, with his hands stretched towards the water bucket; the very goblet they drank from slowly ascended out of the bucket with water in it, floated a foot above the bucket, and moved into the priest's stretched out hands as he lowered his face and looked to it. The gods, not men, are fit to administer an oath to a priest. And the gods did so before the eyes of these terrified honorable men.

Having taken oath, the 9 members of this secret assembly moved to discuss Gold Coast independence, the request by certain members of the legislature to have Britain replace its Gold Coast governor, and Italy's attack on Abyssinia's sovereignty.

During the first point of discussion, the secret assembly concluded that the second discussion was needless. If one governor was disapproving of the proposition of an independent Gold Coast nation, a new governor is only likely to follow suit, they agreed. It was hardly the governor's plans executed here in their land; Great Britain birthed and hatched the plans, and the governor merely executed the crown's prearrangements. Consequentially, they had to demand of Britain their independence, which will ensure self-rule. The party of 9, summarily, concluded a careful plan – gradual procession to independence that should include increment of intellectual locals in the administration, the creation of a constitution that makes for a broad-based legislature, a separation of tribal and cultural government from mainstream politics, and the relinquishing of more cabinet positions to the locals by the British.

On the third and final discussion, the 9 members discussed various possibilities to get Great Britain going to the aid of Abyssinia. They sought, first, to determine any leverage they may have in this negotiation. And second, to establish the possibilities of same for the colonial power. For a considerably long while their deliberations showed the scale of leverage lay against them. A pause followed. Then, lifting his face out of his hands, with his eyes lighted as certainly from a breakthrough of thought, Sir Theophilus Quartey broke the silence:

"Gentlemen, you might have perceived it strange and farfetched from reality that we could successfully oppose sending out our military troop into the service of Great Britain. I must assure you it is possible, and the consequence cannot be any more spiteful than is already meted us by the British. Even more contrarily, we are at an advantage now that the Brits fights to protect themselves in Europe, and her interests in faraway nations across Asia and Africa. Germany appears to have the upper hand in Europe, and Russia can be no trusted ally of these imperialists. Everything – material and human resources will be heavily required in the war (WWII). With the United States reluctance, Africa is Britain's best hope to maintain a kingdom at home and a commonwealth across the world. Yes, the blood of our young men, and the gold, iron ore and timber of our land will be instrumental to our ma-sters (the words broke as though from pain or disgust).

"Our venerable priest here has been influential in bringing Ashanti into the Gold Coast. The underlying purpose, everyone present should know, is to unite and strengthen our whole peoples toward an independent democratic state. And pointless will be an independent Gold Coast if a foreign power holds a single people under colonial rule. We shall therefore make our case to the British governor: *Every local serving in the British Gold Coast government, the British Ashanti Protectorate, the chiefs and elders, and every common citizen, will work with our resources as it befits all parties' common interest, predicate on Britain's support for Ethiopia, couple with a genuine formal pledge to accept, recognize and ally with us when it becomes apparently crystal that the peoples now forming a common interest as a state under the Gold Coast can rule themselves."*

The 10 X 12 room and its shut window and door stood no chance of suppressing the cheers from the priest and other legislators. Finally, and here is hope. The hope of one African nation depended on the other, and every one on Liberia and Ethiopia, the only republics on the African continent. This hope would thread dangerous waters, but the speaker knew the time was now or never. And so did his honorable comrades and the magnificent priest.

With deliberations reaching decisions and committees set up, the 9 men concluded their secret meeting. Their hopes are reasonably high, but they understand the sacrifices required and are willing to commit thereto. They reckon it will demand many others the likes of themselves, but they are prepared to meticulously recruit others into the assembly. And of time and chance, it is fitly observed by one of the legislators: *"Every day that sees us atop the earth presents us chance – countless many chances, but it is our responsibilities to identify what chance is meted out to us, in consideration of time."* Having acknowledged all that is at stake, the 9 men shook hands, hugged, and patted each other's backs, before departing the humble house. From 9:03AM to sometime after 6:00PM, the men could not be more pleased with their commitments.

All of the men returned home with great joy, but a greater sense of responsibility appeared to overshadow it or make one cautious upon reflections. Sir Theophilus Quartey found it no different. In fact, the responsibility weighed on him more than any member of that assembly. He will decide possible names of people to talk to, probable times, as well as traveling and informing his comrades. Hence, Sir Quartey retired to bed and found himself in a meeting with Sir Arnold Weinholt Hodson, Governor of the Gold Coast. And to his great surprise, the governor was apathetic to his several concerns, though unable in the most part, to help. Not as much as Sir Quartey would hope for, but that was a dream. Just a dream, Sir Quartey had told himself.

Over the month following, the members of the secret assembly met several times. And they held meetings with fellow Gold Coast Assembly members, and British officials of Gold Coast, including the governor Sir Arnold Weinholt Hodson. The governor and his team of imperial representatives had advised Sir Theophilus Quartey and his fellows to send a delegation to Buckingham, London, and plead with the British Crown. He offered to arrange the meeting, to which Sir Quartey and his associates were delighted. It was not an assurance the governor had stressed, but for these men, it was a chance. At the least, there is hope for Abyssinia and Africa and the British Gold Coast. There is hope for an independent Africa.

On 5th January 1936, at 16:00GMT, a three-man delegation from the British Gold Coast in West Africa arrives in London. By 16:50, they are seated at 10 Downing Street, London SW1A 2AA. Their host is Stanley Baldwin, 1st Earl of Bewdley and Prime Minister of Great Britain. He will listen to the delegates and confer with the Crown – King George V. The king is gravely ill, and is unlikely to meet the men directly. But the King or the Prime Minister, for these men, all that matter is England committing to support of Abyssinia. A British Commonwealth support for Abyssinia and Africa.

A week later, Theophilus Quartey and his men arrived back home. England showed sympathy towards their plight, but would commit to no action that might jeopardize its own security from Italy and Germany at home and abroad. The British economy was only just recovering and the government was concentrating a good portion of its revenue on arms, in reaction to possible Nazi invasion. Therefore, with Germany and Italy having united, the British, like their French counterparts, are in a fix. To support Abyssinia was to risk their empires. Hence, in spite Britain's detestation of Italian occupation of the East African empire, it could not allow sympathy to exceed its direct interest. The three-man delegates may not have agreed with their colonial master, but at least they understand the realistic consequences a British support for the African empire might incur. The men returned to their country and their homes, hoping for a twist of fate that might change the political landscape of the world to favor the Black Continent.

About four years after their ineffective trip to London, the men of the Secret Assembly had something to celebrate. The World War II had arrived at a decisive point for Africa. British interests in Africa was attacked by the Italians. British and Commonwealth troops Somaliland, Kenya and Sudan came under Italian attacks. As a result, by 1941, the Britain mobilized its forces and made major assaults against Italy in Abyssinia.

Nana Yaw Edusei Berimah was a member of the British Gold Coast troop that formed part of the 11th African Division under British General Harry Edward de Robillard Wetherall. On April 6, 1941 the capital Addis Ababa was captured by the 11th African Division, and on May 5th, the Abyssinian emperor Haile Selassie returned to his capital, following five years of Italian occupation.

Within his first month of return from exile, Emperor Haile Selassie entertained seven political leaders from 5 African countries. The men sought to welcome the emperor back to his throne, pledge their support, and strategize the security and liberation of the greater African continent. Two of the seven dignitaries, Sir Theophilus Kwakwei Quartey and Hon. Ekow Kutu-Adu of the British Gold Coast were involved in several intervention meetings with British, French and other African officials for Abyssinia. Though every one of those meetings concluded unsuccessfully, the men were glad that at least fate played to their advantage. The British finally came to Abyssinia's aid because she was attacked by the common enemy – Italy. But the men are here in Addis Ababa, the capital of Abyssinia, along with their Liberian, Nigerian, Egyptian, and Tanzanian counterparts to design an alliance for African independence, security, and economy. It is evident they cannot rely on Britain or any colonial power for their security and economy; Africans are Africa's only hope.

At the close of that seven days retreat, the Gold Coast officials, in connection with the local British representatives, provided 10 men from the British Gold Coast contingent in Abyssinia to handle personal security for the emperor.

Among the 10 men from the British Gold Coast contingent to provide protection for Emperor Haile Selassie was Nana Yaw Edusei Berimah. The only child of Nana Serwaa Berimah, the boy was born with an adventurous nature. In his early teenage, before going to the Ashanti Royal Military Academy, the boy dared and conquered. He hunted wildlife, accomplished great feats at swimming, running and several other physical and athletic games. But beyond his physical prowess, the young Yaw excelled in academics. In whatever the boy did, he stood out. Many in Oman and Ashanti early on called him a child of the gods.

Here in the east African empire, the young Nana Yaw will command nine of his comrades, and eventually the entire royal guards. Leadership and first place has always belonged to him. Or rather, he has always worked toward that, and whether consciously or unconsciously, no one could be certain. For the man never admitted to being ambitious.

Nana Yaw Berimah had been in Abyssinia over a year. It has been all soldiery these 13 months. And so it is expected to be for time indefinite. Put mildly, yet still demanding, until the empire is at peace and its neighbors are liberated from colonial rule. Yaw Berimah has pledged his life to his professional career, but time will test him like it does every soldier. To be away from one's family and in a strange land for a year is a hard task. And he knows it is likely to get harder, not easy. It will necessitate a lot emotionally, and though this Akan's biological make may project a magnificent emotional balance, it must be observed that he, too, is human. Yet, it is time and events that will determine the quality of the man and his makeup.

As Emperor Haile Selassie settles back in at his flamboyant and newly built Guenete Leul Palace (Paradise of Princes), security will be of inestimable priority. The emperor has personally met with the Gold Coast soldiers, and within the first week addressed everyone by name. It was somewhat unsurprising to these men, for they had monitored radio as a duty, and were abreast with the great oratory skill of the emperor. It is expected that a great speaker will have an impressive recollection. And the first week was a long enough time for the great man to prove himself worthy of the West Africans expectations of him.

Days turned into week, and weeks into month. In the second month, when Emperor Selassie's top aide was removed for guilt of conspiracy against the emperor, Nana Berimah was promoted to the vacancy. In that meeting, the ruler put a rhetorical question to the soldier. "Tell me, Yaw. What will you do, if you were ruler of this fragile empire, and your trusted most aide, who eats at your table, conspires against you? And take into consideration your decision will set a precedent against possible future conspirators, or lay the basis for sequences of conspiracies that will destroy the very fabric of identities that bind us as a people, and plunge the empire into perpetual chaos and war."

With a reverential bow of the head, Yaw Berimah started "Um...Your Majesty. A branch that is diseased need must be plucked out from the tree in order to preserve the whole tree. A man capable of taking away his master's life does himself deserve the death. For, if my chief aide should have the opportunity and the gods show me no mercy, he will proceed with his deed and I would be no more. Therefore, if the gods lay bare his deeds before me, he will die the death that I may live. Your Majesty..." The soldier bowed once more, this time much slowly.

"You are a just man, and appear much younger than your great wisdom" the monarch admonished Yaw Berimah. "The news of my now deceased aide is no secret from you. From today, I make you my chief aide. You and your team are accountable for my personal security, and you have nobody but myself to report to. Palus, the Palace Minister, will make available to you as many men as you may require; within 72 hours, I want the entire palace guards replaced, and without notice to them." At that the emperor motioned with his left hand releasing his chief aide from his presence. As the soldier jumped to his feet and bowed, the Abyssinian ruler called to him in a rather supportive and personal tone "A man cannot live without a woman, and yet, it is the moral man that keeps his purse and his head. You need a wife. She can be of great help to you." The new head of imperial security could only nod, confused about a response as he was caught off guard by His Majesty's interjection of an intimate matter during what until now appeared an official meeting.

On a warm Friday evening, three months following the Emperor's return, Palus invited Yaw Berimah to dinner in the upper staff dining room within the Guenete Leul Palace. The white painted concrete walls and rich marble floor helped illuminated the space this twilight. The host reached to the windows and drew the curtains, while a young woman standing at the head of the table began lighting the candles. The palace minister returned to the center of the room and invited his guest to a seat immediate left of the head chair. He took seat opposite his guest, while the woman sat at the head. Then Palus beckoned to her and pointed to the emperor's chief aide, "Captain Yaw Berimah, new head of His Majesty security," and returned reversed the act, "Gelila, daughter of His Majesty's cousin." The Captain rose to his feet, and so did the Lady Gelila, greeting each other with respect and warmth. As they sat again, each had made tremendous effort to conceal his thought. Yaw wrestled to hide his confusion, and the Lady struggled to mask her knowledge of this arrangement. Thanks to the Minister who ushered dinner underway, the pair redirected their focus to the meal before them.

An hour of food and drink and talks of Abyssinia and the royal family went by swiftly. Yaw Berimah could listen on and on, and Palus and Gelila could speak of the legends of Abyssinia forever, and the mysticism of the imperial family eternally. But the minister requested leave, and standing to his feet, spoke "Gelila here will be your wife, my friend. His Majesty has given you her hand, and the priest will bless your union in two days." With those words he excused the couple.

They sat and looked at each other and the table and decors and walls intermittently. After about two minutes of silence, Yaw Berimah braved the storm, manning to the occasion. He encouraged the Lady that marital arrangement was not the least alien to his native culture. In fact, it is such a union that accounts for his birth. He told her of his parents and himself, and when he was done, she almost doubted that such a great young man did not leave a wife home. But she saw the truth of every word reflect from his eyes by the candle light. She is impressed with his childhood adventures and professional accomplishments, and relieved to know that the choosing of her uncle bears noble blood. However, she is startled to find that Yaw Berimah has discussed nothing of his family with the emperor, and yet the man His Majesty chooses for her is a prince.

Nana Yaw Edusei Berimah hurt both his parents and the people of Oman when he decided against becoming ruler of the kingdom. The people endured much hurt and many disappointment leading up to his birth, though not any near his mother. They banished his mother because their need for a male child of the Berimah superseded their love for Nana Serwaa. They loved her dearly, but even that love had its origin in Oman's eternal bond to the Berimah's. They regretted and apologized for all they put her through, though they will never know the whole. And that shameful pain his mother endured, which she had voice to tell only him, has put him at odds with the kingdom. She had interceded with him for Oman, but the boy can never find it in his heart to pardon and rule the very people that inflicted on or caused so great suffering for his mother. At least, for the young Yaw, forgiveness did not include residing in or ruling Oman.

When Gelila gave birth to a son less than a year after their marriage, she requested to see Yaw Berimah's parents and kingdom. She decided it was time for him to reunite with his people, and that she was prepared to move over with him. But he gave her the obvious excuse of being on an assignment. He is a member of the British Gold Coast contingent in the empire, and it is improbable to desert his duty, and dishonorable to request a leave while the World War II continues. Besides, he is apprehensive that a return to Oman, especially with his family, they might compel him to be king. Indeed, Oman will never permit his stay in the kingdom as an ordinary citizen. She could understand his stay in Abyssinia and accepted it was appropriate. But she insisted that "it is unfair to live with hate against one's own people, and cowardice to flee any innate office of destiny. It is as much as disbelieving and rejecting one's own existence." And reluctantly, he had promised that when the war was over, hewill return to Oman with her and their son.

16 years earlier, when Yaw Edusei returned home from the Ashanti Royal Military Academy, Oman was preparing for war. Wa-Zanga, it became known, coerced Oman, and Asahnti subsequently, into the alliance. The Great League was founded on deception. Tuoza, who was Oman's Ambassador to the League and General Secretary thereof, uncovered the shocking information that Wa-Zanga was behind the so-called Indemba capture of Nana Serwaa. And then, it purported to commit men and resources for the freedom of the princess.

With Nana Yaw Edusei sick and physically incapacitated, Oman looks to its prince and expected king Nana Yaw Edusei Berimah to lead her to war against Wa-Zanga. 25,000 men have been mobilized across Oman and Ashanti and the neighboring countries. And Indemba, betrayed of Wa-Zanga, is lending intelligence and other forms of support to the Omanian planned invasion.

Two days before the Omanian led army macrh on Wa-Zanga, Nana Serwaa informed her son that he will become king upon his return from the battle. The young man will love to lay waste Wa-Zanga, but he cannot accept to become ruler over the kingdom. He is afraid that these people are careless of the Berimah's office, or at least their customs and traditions made no guaranteed provision for their protection. And because he cannot predict the future, he wishes to live his life away from his people.

The next day the prince was nowhere to be found. Before sunset, Nana Serwaa sat in a meeting with all of Oman's top officials, including the sick governor and Tuoza. She explained her son's position and possible reason for deserting his duties to the Omanian army. And there, to their astonishment, she pledged to lead them to battle against Wa-Zanga tomorrow. It was a decision, they all knew, and not a proposition. She requested that all preparations and plans continue without change or adjustment. When she was done speaking, she helped her husband out of the meeting.

The princess and governor spent the entire evening and night within the walls of the governor's chamber. They reminisced of their younger days, particularly the first months of their marriage. Of course, the couple's love is strong as always, but great times have not been any commonplace in their relationship. And then, with their reunion and boy child came Yaw's partial paralysis as a result of stroke. But tonight, they check those great moments, unconcerned about the numerous setbacks their relationship have suffered. Not even the fleeing of their son matters tonight. It is their night, perhaps their last night together, and they will celebrate. She will be his immobile right hand and feeble right leg, and in the heat of their love, the intensity of their passion, as romance sing aloud and their bodies dance, they burn, they burn, they burn and are consumed. Then, as always, the morning mystery of their phoenixic revival transpired. And the princess, after readying for battle, kissed Yaw and walked out of the chamber without a word. They said it all during the night. Today, she must maintain her courage and lead her people into battle. Return or not, her soul will rejoice, knowing that as best she could, she stood up against an enemy that sought to destroy she and her people. But if the gods be favorable to her cause, then she shall rejoice in life, and her soul later in death.

At first light Nana Serwaa met with Tuoza her counselor, who has become, again, the Court Administrator, and her army chief and treasurer. They all furnished her with reports on tasks they were obligated to completing for this offensive. Everything went according to plan, and the princess is highly impressed. He commends the men for the quality and efficiency of the job executed. Yet the princess is aware that the ordinary soldiers are the ones she must lift her wits and speak to. She learned early from her father to appeal to the hearts of the soldiers, and not their minds. The muster is all set, and she addresses over 5,000 Omanians who will lead the allied force against Wa-Zanga.

She greeted the troop and raised a war chant to which they responded mightily. Then, after a second's pause, Nana Serwaa continued on:

"My father used to say that there are no people mightier than our people, and wiser than the children of this land. He led you to many battles, and he found that those true of you Omanians. And what do I say more? There are no people more loving than you, for in spite our differences of recent past, the great love you demonstrated for me in my exile will live for eternity. Your sacrifices I carry in my heart as a priceless treasure.

To every man that lifted the hand in war my father gave an ounce of gold; but today, the royal coffers affords you two. For every Omanian soldier that fell in battle, my father demanded two of the enemy; but, men of Oman, I demand 5, and more so, I demand total annihilation of Wa-Zanga. Except that kingdom is wiped from the face of the earth, everyone here present and your families, and your generations to come, will bear the shame of Wa-Zanga insults.

I know the men I make this demand of. And yet, not I, but your wives and children, and Nana Berimah your king! As we go against those barbarians, I will lead you, with the spirit of my father, your king! And the gods of our fathers be with us!"

Within 18 days, Nana Serwaa returned home with the troop. She led them to the war as a princess, but upon their return, Oman had asked her to become queen. They found, by experience, that there is no distinction between any mighty man and Nana Serwaa. She was wise and strong. She had just led them in the utter destruction of Wa-Zanga. By her very hands King Buka encountered his horrifying end, and the men with her stood petrified. When the Omnians left Wa-Zanga, there was not a living, human or beast.

Yaw Berimah traveled with the Emperor Haile Selassie to the latter's home town of Ejersa Goro. Before their departure that morning, Yaw took off a beaded bracelet from his hand and put it on the baby's. He kissed both child and mother and promised to see them soon. About two hours after the Emperor's convoy left the palace, to Gelila's and all of the royal family residing in the palace shocking amazement, Halie's convoy returned. But fewer cars and wounded men only indicated that the emperor and his entourage had come under attack. His chief Aide and head of security Yaw lost his life shielding him. Many years ago he escaped his kingdom a coward, but today, in a foreign land, Nana Yaw Edusei Berimah goes to the grave a hero.

Yaw Berimah was ever reluctant to return to his parents and kingdom. Whatever accounts for his reluctance, one may safely ascribe it to the gods: the gods did not will it. Or, more bluntly, that the gods appointed his end in Abyssinia. And his wife Gelila will mourn him her entire life, and his son will never know him. There is no returning to his mother, and his ailing father will go to the grave without seeing his son's bright eyes again.

5 years after the death of her husband, Gelila traces him back to his kingdom. Yaw's death have only intensified her need to visit his kingdom and meet with his parent. She pray the gods keep them alive. For what is the joy of life for her little boy if he never sees his father, and worse, never know with certainty his paternal land of nativity and kinsmen. She is therefore determined to go to the ends of the earth, if her pursuit demands.

8:00 AM GMT, July 26, 1947, Emperor Haile Selassie, accompanied by his niece Gelila arrives in Liberia for its centennial Independence Day celebration. Gelila travels with her son Nana Adunga Berimah. After the Liberian celebration, the emperor will drop them off in British Gold Coast before heading home. The pair seek the rulers of Oman. They desire answers to questions that will give peace to Gelila and joy to her kid. She will call on the Edusei house in Ashanti and the Berimah's in Oman.

From the Gold Coast to Ashanti – Kumasi took an 11 hours' drive. The House of Edusei was contacted about visitors from Abyssinia, and hurriedly came to receive their son and in-law. A son was important in Ashanti culture, therefore Gelila got a princess' welcome. In their days in Kumasi, they had audience with the new king of Ashanti Otumfuo Nana Osei Tutu Agyeman Prempeh II, Ashantehene. And several members of the Berituos – the Ashanti ruling family to which Nana Yaw Edusei belonged, brought gifts for the kid and his mother. It was a delightful experience in Ashanti, except the news of her father-in-law's illness troubled Gelila.

The road to Oman is still limited to carriages or walking. It will take a few years before cars reach the kingdom. Gelila wonders what it looks like, since there is not a road for car. But that is of little concern to the Abyssinian. The Ashantehene had assigned her one of his finely decorated carriages pulled by two black stallions. The carriage interior was colorful with hand crafted seat cover designed with pearls and molten gold. The exterior was a mix of lion's skin and the same richly colored kente cloth that made up the interior covering. From half a mile the golden yellow, red, green and black exterior is visible. The Royal Palace in Kumasi boosted dozens of these carriages and hundreds of fine stallions.

The journey to Oman seemed eternally long. Five days went by, then, on the sixth, at dusk, Gelila and her son arrived on Omanian soil, escorted by 18 Ashanti soldiers. Soon, the villages were behind them, and they rode through the main city street until they came up to the palace. Queen Nana Serwaa and her husband Yaw Edusei were in the living room playing a game of Oware over tea when a servant came in and announced the guests. Old Yaw struggled to his feet, and so did the queen, before the latter called out to the servant to usher in his grandson and daughter-in-law.

As Gelila stepped into the sitting room with her son, they found themselves in the embraces of an old man and an ageing woman. Then Nana Serwaa lifted the kid into her arms, and stood by her husband as they admired their grandson. The Queen had to lift the boy because Yaw had only one capable hand, and a single fully functioning leg. In a moment, they took seats, had the guests served water as tradition demanded, and conversation was underway.

Of course, inquiry about Gelila and the boys travel were simply formalities, and that the Abyssinian woman knew. It is obvious that the old couple will love Adunga, but what about their son? She journeyed this far, putting off all those moments how to confront the question of her husband. Now it stares her in the eyes, and she must gather her wits.

"Yaw Berimah... where is he?" the Queen asked. "Your Majesty..." Gelila exhaled noticeably. The two officials of the royal court, along with the Queen and Governor, watched their guest with anxious eyes and listened with somewhat impatience as the young woman struggled to answer. "Yaw is dead" she said, almost whispering. The living room went dead for several seconds, before weeping was heard. Mother and father wept for their son, wife wept for her husband, and an innocent child looked on in confusion. As other relatives entered the room and the weeping continued, a female servant took the kid from the midst of the mourners. Nana Serwaa mourned and could not be comforted. The governor, unable to weep anymore, sat on the floor and grieved.

But by day break, the Queen and Governor are alarmed. Oman had not come to mourn with them. No official has visited the royal family, except the two men that had escorted Gelila and her son to the palace yesterday. It is obvious. As Nana Serwaa Berimah sat alone in her room that morning, she cried uncontrollably. This time only she does not mourn for her dead son, but cries for Oman's rejection of her grandson. The interpretation of her subjects' actions can mean nothing more or less.

Her son abandoned Oman during the Wa-Zanga battle. But did she not lead them in the very battle and gave them victory? Did they crown her Queen because of her father? Certainly not. Oman saw her on the battlefield, a fearless and daring woman that they claimed was possessed by the god of war. And before they had returned home, they unanimously decided and elevated her from a princess to Queen. They came to believe that a woman can rule a kingdom no less than a man. And the years since, the economy has prospered and Omanians are wealthier. Even more, the kingdom has been at peace and Ashanti has recognized its sovereignty; the office of her husband – the governorship has been a mere formality.

In spite of all the progress, Oman turns on her again. It may be they are afraid a child born of a strange woman may rule over them. Nana Serwaa, in her heart, would love to see her grandson succeed her. She has non other to succeed her and it is an open fact for these people. Even worse, the boy is the very offspring of the coward Yaw Berimah who abandoned the kingdom and fled before the Wa-Zangan war.

At 57, the Queen is unable to walk those miles she did during her banishment. Her husband is old and sick, and she cannot trust her kinsmen and officials. Her grandson's life is at risk, and he is only a child, incapable of defending himself. After many hours of deliberations, Nana Serwaa Berimah and her husband decide to move back Kumasi.

On the morning of their departure to Kumasi, Nana Adunga Berimah could not be woken from bed. Neither could his mother. They were dead, not asleep. And, hearing this, the Queen fell off in her bed. The royal house sat at her bedside while a doctor sought to revive her. An hour went by. Two hours. Then, on the third, she was revived. As she opened her eyes and saw her family sit around her bed, she closed her eyes and silently asked the gods "why did you restore me? Why do you not spare me this suffering? Who else have buried their parents, child and grandchild? Where is your sword!?"

Printed in the United States
By Bookmasters